Daphne had braced herself for an argument about how he was the crown prince, blah, blah, blah....

Instead, Murat had simply nodded and said, "As you wish." Then he'd left, leaving Daphne with a very restless night ahead of her.

While she told herself she should be happy that Murat was finally seeing reason, she didn't trust the man. Certainly not his last cryptic agreement. As she wished *what?*

After slipping into her robe, she hurried toward the fresh coffee waiting on a cart near the sofa. The steaming liquid perked her up with the first sip. "Better," Daphne said when she'd swallowed half a cup.

She then picked up the folded newspapers. The first was a copy of *USA TODAY*. Underneath was the local Bahanian paper. She flipped it open, then screamed.

For on the front page was a color picture of her under a headline announcing her engagement to Murat....

D0030910

Dear Reader,

Spring might be just around the corner, but it's not too late to curl up by the fire with this month's lineup of six heartwarming stories. Start off with *Three Down the Aisle*, the first book in bestselling author Sherryl Woods's new miniseries, THE ROSE COTTAGE SISTERS. When a woman returns to her childhood haven, the last thing she expects is to fall in love! And make sure to come back in April for the next book in this delightful new series.

Will a sexy single dad find *All He Ever Wanted* in a search-and-rescue worker who saves his son? Find out in Allison Leigh's latest book in our MONTANA MAVERICKS: GOLD RUSH GROOMS miniseries. The Fortunes of Texas are back, and you can read the first three stories in the brand-new miniseries THE FORTUNES OF TEXAS: REUNION, only in Silhouette Special Edition. The continuity launches with *Her Good Fortune* by Marie Ferrarella. Can a straitlaced CEO make it work with a feisty country girl who's taken the big city by storm? Next, don't miss the latest book in Susan Mallery's DESERT ROGUES ongoing miniseries, *The Sheik & the Bride Who Said No*. When two former lovers reunite, passion flares again. But can they forgive each other for past mistakes? Be sure to read the next book in Judy Duarte's miniseries, BAYSIDE BACHELORS. A fireman discovers his ex-lover's child is *Their Secret Son*, but can they be a family once again? And pick up Crystal Green's *The Millionaire's Secret Baby*. When a ranch chef lands her childhood crush—and tycoon—can she keep her identity hidden, or will he discover her secrets?

Enjoy, and be sure to come back next month for six compelling new novels, from Silhouette Special Edition.

All the best,

Gail Chasan
Senior Editor

Please address questions and book requests to:
Silhouette Reader Service
U.S.: 3010 Walden Ave., P.O. Box 1325, Buffalo, NY 14269
Canadian: P.O. Box 609, Fort Erie, Ont. L2A 5X3

Susan Mallery

THE SHEIK & THE BRIDE WHO SAID NO

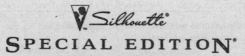

Silhouette

SPECIAL EDITION

Published by Silhouette Books

America's Publisher of Contemporary Romance

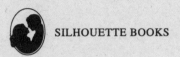 SILHOUETTE BOOKS

ISBN 0-373-24666-8

THE SHEIK & THE BRIDE WHO SAID NO

Visit Silhouette Books at www.eHarlequin.com

Printed in U.S.A.

Books by Susan Mallery

SUSAN MALLERY

is the bestselling and award-winning author of over fifty books for Harlequin and Silhouette Books. She makes her home in the Los Angeles area with her handsome prince of a husband and her two adorable-but-not-bright cats. Feel free to contact her via her Web site at www.susanmallery.com.

Chapter One

"I know marrying the crown prince and eventually being queen *sounds* terrific," Daphne Snowden said in what she hoped was a calm I'm-your-aunt-who-loves-you-and-I-know-better voice instead of a shrill, panicked tone. "But the truth of the matter is very different. You've never met Prince Murat. He's a difficult and stubborn man."

Daphne knew this from personal experience. "He's also nearly twice your age."

Brittany looked up from the fashion magazine she'd been scanning. "You worry too much," she said. "Relax, Aunt Daphne. I'll be fine."

Fine? Fine? Daphne sank back into the comfortable

leather seat of the luxury private jet and tried not to scream. This could not be happening. It was a dream. It had to be. She refused to believe that her favorite— and only—niece had agreed to marry a man she'd never met. Prince or no prince, this could be a disaster. Despite the fact that she and Brittany had been having the same series of conversations for nearly three weeks now, she felt compelled to make all her points again.

"I want you to be happy," Daphne said. "I love you."

Brittany, a tall willowy blonde with delicately pretty features in the tradition of the Snowden women, smiled. "I love you, too, and you're worrying about nothing. I know Murat is, like, really old."

Daphne pressed her lips together and tried not to wince. She knew that to an eighteen-year-old, thirty-five was practically geriatric, but it was only five years beyond her own thirty years.

"But he's pretty cute," her niece added. "And rich. I'll get to travel and live in a palace." She put down the magazine and stuck out her feet. "Do you think I should have gone with the other sandals instead of these?"

Daphne held in a shriek. "I don't care about your shoes. I'm talking about your *life* here. Being married to the crown prince means you won't get to spend your day shopping. You'll have responsibilities for the welfare of the people of Bahania. You'll have to entertain visiting dignitaries and support charities. You'll be expected to produce children."

Brittany nodded. "I figured that part out. The parties

will be great. I can invite all my friends, and we'll talk about, like, what the guy who runs France is wearing."

"And the baby part?"

Brittany shrugged. "If he's old, he probably knows what he's doing. My friend Deanna had sex with her college boyfriend and she said it was totally better than with her boyfriend in high school. Experience counts."

Daphne wanted to shake Brittany. She knew from dozens of after-midnight conversations, when her niece had spent the night, that Brittany had never been intimate with any of her boyfriends. Brittany had been very careful not to let things go too far. So what had changed? Daphne couldn't believe that the child she'd loved from birth and had practically raised, could have turned into this shallow, unfeeling young woman.

She glanced at her watch and knew that time was running short. Once they landed and reached the palace, there would be no turning back. One Snowden bride-to-be had already left Murat practically at the altar. She had a feeling that Brittany wouldn't be given the opportunity to bolt.

"What was your mother thinking?" she asked, more to herself than Brittany. "Why did she agree?"

"Mom thought it would be completely cool," Brittany said easily. "I think she's hoping there will be some amazing jewelry for the mother of the bride. Plus me marrying a prince beats out Aunt Grace's piggy Justin getting into Harvard any day, right?"

Daphne nodded without speaking. Some families were competitive about sports while others kept score using social status and money. In her family it was all about power—political or otherwise. One of her sisters had married a senator who planned to run for president, the other married a captain of industry. She had been the only sibling to pick another path.

She scooted to the edge of her seat and took Brittany's perfectly manicured hands into her own.

"You have to listen," she said earnestly. "I love you more than I've ever loved another human being in my life. You're practically my daughter."

Brittany's expression softened. "I love you, too. You know you've been there for me way more than my own mother."

"Then, please, please, think this through. You're young and smart and you can have anything you want in the world. Why would you be willing to tie yourself to a man you've never met in a country you've never visited? What if you hate Bahania?"

Daphne didn't think that was possible—personally she loved the desert country—but at this point she was done playing fair.

"Travel isn't going to be what you think," Daphne continued before Brittany could interrupt. "Any visits will be state events. They'll be planned and photographed. Once you agree to marry the prince you'll never be able to just run over and see a girlfriend or head to the mall or the movies."

Brittany stared at her. "What do you mean I can't go to the mall?"

Daphne blinked. Was this progress at last? "You'll be

the future queen. You won't be able to rush off and buy a last-minute cashmere sweater just because it's on sale."

"Why not?"

Daphne sighed. "I've been trying to explain this to you. You won't get to be your own person anymore. You'll be living a life in a foreign country with unfamiliar rules and expectations. You will have to adhere to them."

None of which sounded all that tough to her, but she wasn't the one signing up for a lifetime of queenhood.

"I never thought about having to stay in the palace a lot," Brittany said slowly. "I just sort of figured I could fly back home whenever I wanted and hang with my friends."

"Bahania will be your home now."

Brittany's eyes darkened. "I wouldn't miss Mom and Dad so much, but Deanna and you." She bit her lower lip. "I guess if I love the prince…"

"Do you?" Daphne asked. "You've never met him. You're risking a whole lot on the off chance you two will get along." She squeezed her niece's fingers. "You've only had a couple of boyfriends, none of them serious. Do you really want to give all that up? Dating? College?"

Brittany frowned. "I can't go to college?"

"Do you think any professor is going to want the future queen in his class? How could he or she give you a real grade? Even if you did get that worked out, you'd just be attending classes part-time. You couldn't live on campus."

"That's right. Because I'd be in the palace."

"Possibly pregnant," Daphne added for good measure.

"No way. I'm not ready to have a baby *now*."

"And if Prince Murat is?"

Her niece glared at her. "You're trying to scare me."

"You bet. I'm willing to do just about anything to keep you from throwing away your life. If you'd met someone and had fallen in love, then I wouldn't care if he was a prince or an alien from planet Xeon. But you didn't. I would have gotten involved with this sooner, but your mother did her best to keep the truth from me."

Brittany sighed. "She's pretty determined to have her way."

"I'm not going to let that happen. Tell me honestly. Tell me you're completely committed to this and I'll back off. But if you have even one hint of a doubt, you need to give yourself time to think."

Brittany swallowed. "I'm not sure," she admitted in a tiny voice. "I want things to go great with the prince, but what if they don't?" Tears filled her eyes. "I've been trying to do what my parents want me to do and I'm scared." She glanced around the luxury plane. "The pilot said we were landing in twenty minutes. That's about up. I can't meet the prince and tell him I'm not sure."

Daphne vowed that when she returned to the States she was going to kill her oldest sister, Laurel. How dare she try to guilt her only daughter into something like this? Outrage mingled with relief. She held open her arms, and Brittany fell into her embrace.

"Is it too late?" the teenager asked.

"Of course not. You're going to be fine." She hugged

her tight. "You had me worried for a while. I thought you were really going through with this."

Brittany sniffed. "Some parts of it sounded pretty fun. Having all that money and crowns and stuff, but I tried not to think about actually being married to someone that old."

"I don't blame you." The age difference was impossible, Daphne thought. What on earth could Murat be thinking, considering an engagement to a teenager?

"I'll take care of everything," she promised. "You'll stay on the plane and go directly home while I handle things at the palace."

Brittany straightened. "Really? I don't even have to meet him?"

"Nope. You go back and pretend this never happened."

"What about Mom?"

Daphne's eyes narrowed. "You can leave her to me, as well."

Just over an hour later Daphne found herself in the back of a limo, heading to the fabled Pink Palace of Bahania. Because of the long plane trip, she expected to find the city in darkness, but with the time difference, it was late afternoon. She sat right by the window so she could take in everything—the ancient buildings that butted up against the new financial district. The amazing blue of the Arabian Sea just south of the city. The views were breathtaking and familiar. She'd grown to love this country when she'd visited ten years ago.

"Don't go there," she told herself. There was no time for a trip down memory lane. Instead she needed to focus and figure out what she was going to say to Murat.

She glanced at her watch. With every second that ticked by, finding the perfect words became less and less important. Once Brittany landed back in the States, she would be safe from Murat's clutches. Still, she couldn't help feeling a little nervous as the long, black car turned left and drove past elegant wrought-iron gates.

The car pulled to a stop in front of the main entrance. Daphne drew in a deep breath to calm herself as she waited for one of the guards to open the door. She stepped out into the warm afternoon and glanced around.

The gardens were as beautiful as she remembered. Sweet, lush scents competed for her attention. To the left was the gate that led to the private English-style garden she'd always loved. To the right was a path that led to the most perfect view of the sea. And in front of her...well, that was the way into the lion's den.

She tried to tell herself she had no reason to be afraid, that she'd done nothing wrong. Murat was the one interested in marrying a teenager nearly half his age. If anyone should be feeling foolish and ashamed, it was he.

But despite being in the right, and determined to stand strong against any and all who might try to get in her way, she couldn't help a tiny shiver of apprehension. After all, ten years ago she'd been a guest in this very palace. She'd been young and in love and engaged to be married.

To Murat.

Then three weeks before the wedding, she'd bolted, leaving him without even a whisper of an explanation.

Chapter Two

"Ms. Snowden?"

Daphne saw a well-dressed young man walking toward her. "Yes?"

"The prince is waiting. If you will follow me?"

As Daphne trailed after the man, she wondered if he had any idea she wasn't Brittany. She doubted Murat had bothered to brief his staff on the arrival of a potential bride. He'd rarely concerned himself with details like that. So she would guess that his staff member had simply been told to escort the woman who arrived to an appropriate meeting area.

"Someone is in for a surprise," she murmured under her breath as she walked down a wide corridor lined with stunning mosaics and elegant antiques.

Just being back in the palace made her feel better. She wanted to ask her guide to wait a few minutes while she stopped to enjoy an especially beautiful view from a window or a spectacular piece of artwork. Instead she trailed along dutifully, concentrating on tapestries and carvings instead of what she was going to say when she saw Murat.

They turned a corner. Up ahead Daphne saw a large tabby cat sitting in a patch of sun and washing her face. She smiled as she recalled the dozens and dozens of cats the king kept in the palace.

"In here, Ms. Snowden," the man said as he paused in front of an open door. "The prince will be with you shortly."

She nodded, then walked past him into a small sitting room. The furniture was Western, complete with a sofa, three chairs, a coffee table and a buffet along the far wall. A carafe of ice water and several glasses sat next to a phone on the buffet. She walked over and helped herself to the refreshment.

As she drank she looked around the room and shook her head. How like Murat to have a stranger bring his prospective bride to a room and then drop her off. If Brittany had been here, the teenager would have been terrified by now. The least he could have done was to have sent a woman and then have her keep Brittany company.

But she wasn't Brittany, Daphne reminded herself. Nor was she afraid. Ten years had given her a lot of experience and perspective. Murat might be expecting a young, malleable bride who would bow to his every wish and quiver with fear at the thought of displeasing him, but what he was getting instead was a very different matter.

Footsteps sounded in the hallway. She set down the glass and squared her shoulders. Seconds later the prince from her past strolled into the room.

He still moved with an easy grace of one "to the manor born," she thought as she took in his powerful body and elegant suit. And he was still a formidable opponent, she reminded herself as he stopped and stared at her.

Not by a flicker of a lash did he indicate he was the least bit surprised.

"Daphne," the crown prince said with a slight smile. "You have returned at last."

"I know you weren't expecting me," she said. "But Brittany couldn't make it."

He raised one dark eyebrow. "Has she been taken ill?"

"No. She simply came to her senses. Even as we speak, she's on a plane back to the United States. There isn't going to be a wedding." She thought maybe she'd been a bit abrupt, so she added a somewhat insincere, "I'm sorry."

"Yes, I can feel your compassion from here," Murat said as he crossed to the buffet and picked up the phone. He dialed four numbers, then spoke. "The airport. Flight control."

He waited a few seconds, then spoke again. "My plane?"

She watched while he listened. It was possible a muscle tightened in his jaw, but she couldn't be sure. He had to be feeling something, she told herself. Or maybe not. Ten years ago he'd let her go without a word. Why should this runaway bride matter?

He hung up the phone and turned back to her. "I assume you had something to do with Brittany's decision."

He wasn't asking a question, but she answered it all the same. "Of course. It was madness. I can't imagine what you were thinking. She's barely eighteen, Murat. Still a child. If you're so desperate for a bride, at least pick someone who is close to being an equal."

For the first time since he walked into the room, he showed emotion, and it wasn't a happy one. Temper drew his eyebrows together.

"You insult me with both your familiarity and your assumption."

She winced silently. Of course. She'd called him by his first name. "I apologize for not using the proper title."

"And the other?"

"I'll do whatever is necessary to keep Brittany safe from you."

"Just because you were not interested in being my wife doesn't mean that others feel the same way."

"I agree completely. There is a world filled with willing young women. Have them all—I don't care. But you're not marrying my niece."

Instead of answering her, he pulled a small device out of his pocket. It was about the size of a key fob. Seconds later a half dozen armed guards burst into the room and surrounded Daphne. Two of them grabbed her by the arms.

She was too stunned to protest.

"What are you doing?" she demanded.

"Myself? Nothing." Murat returned what she assumed was a security device to his jacket pocket, then adjusted his cuffs. "The guards are another story."

Daphne glared at him. "What? You're arresting me because I wouldn't let you marry my niece?"

"I'm holding you in protective custody for interfering with the private business of the Crown Prince of Bahania."

She narrowed her gaze. "This is crazy. You can't do this to me."

"All evidence to the contrary."

"Bastard."

She tried to squirm away from the guards, but they didn't let her go.

"You'd better not try to turn that plane around," she said, her fury growing. "I won't let you touch her. Not for a second."

Murat crossed toward the door, then paused and glanced at her. "Make no mistake, Daphne. One way or another, there will be a wedding in four months, and the bride will be a Snowden. There is nothing you can do to stop me."

"Want to bet?" she asked, knowing the words were as futile as her attempt to twist free of the guards.

"Of course. I have no fear of wagering with you." He smiled again. "What will you give me when I win?"

She lunged for him and only got a sharp pain in her arm for her reward. Murat chuckled as he walked away.

"When I get my hands on him," she said. "I swear I'll…" She pressed her lips together. On second thought, threatening the prince while still in the presence of several burly guards wasn't exactly smart.

"Where are you taking me?" she asked when the guards continued to just stand here, holding her in place.

The one by the door touched an earpiece, then nodded.

"What? Getting instructions from the crown prince himself?" she asked. "Couldn't he have told you while he was still in the room?"

Apparently not, she realized as the guards started moving. The two holding on to her kept their grips firm enough that she didn't want to risk pulling away. She had a feeling she was already going to be plenty bruised by her experience.

The group of guards, with her in the center, walked down the main corridor, then stopped at a bank of elevators. The one in communication with Murat pushed the down button. When the car arrived, it was a tight fit, but they all made it inside. Daphne noticed how none of the men stood too close to her. In fact, except for the hold on her arms, they were pretty much ignoring her.

She tried to remember the layout of the palace so she could figure out where they were going. *Down* wasn't her idea of a happy thought. Were there still dungeons in the palace? She wouldn't put it past Murat to lock her up.

But when they stepped out of the elevator and headed along a more narrow corridor, Daphne suddenly realized their destination. It was much worse than any dungeon.

"You're not taking me there," she said, wiggling and twisting to escape.

The guard on her left tightened his grip on her arm. "Ma'am, we don't want to hurt you."

The implication being they would if necessary.

I'll get him for this, she thought as she stopped fighting. One way or another, Murat would pay.

They turned a corner, and Daphne saw the famous gold double doors. They stood nearly ten feet tall and were heavily embossed with a scene of several young women frolicking at an oasis.

One of the guards stepped forward and opened the door on the left. The rest marched her inside.

When the men released her, she thought briefly about making a dash for freedom but knew she would be caught and returned here. So she accepted her fate with dignity and a vow that she would find her way out as soon as she could.

The guards left. She heard the heavy clang as the doors closed behind them and the thunk of the gold cross bar being locked into place. Low conversation from the hallway told her that someone would be left on duty to watch over her.

"This is just like you, Murat," she said as she placed her hands on her hips. "You might be an imperial, piggish prince, but I can stand it. I can stand anything to keep you from marrying Brittany."

Daphne looked for something to throw, but the thick, cream-colored walls were completely bare. The only decoration was the brightly colored tile floor.

She moved through the arched entryway, into the large open living area. Dozens of chairs and sofas filled the vast space. The doorway to the left led to the baths, the one on the right led to the sleeping rooms. She recognized this part of the palace from her explorations ten years before. Recognized and fumed because of it.

Dammit all, if Murat hadn't locked her in the harem.

Murat stalked toward the business wing of the palace. Fury quickened his steps. After all this time Daphne Snowden had dared to return to Bahania, only to once again disrupt his world.

Had she come modestly, begging his apology for her unforgivable acts? Of course not. He swore silently. The woman had stared him in the eye, speaking as if they were equals. She had *defied* him.

Murat swept past the guards outside his father's business suite and stepped into the inner office.

"She is here," he announced as he came to a stop in front of the large, carved desk.

The king raised his eyebrows. "You do not sound happy. Has your fiancée displeased you already?"

"She is not my fiancée."

His father sighed, then stood and walked around the desk. "Murat, I know you have reservations about this engagement. You complain that the girl is too young and inexperienced, that she can never be happy here, but once again I ask you to give her a chance."

Murat stared at his father. Anger bubbled inside of him, although he was careful to keep it from showing. He'd spent a lifetime not reacting to anything, and that practice served him well now.

"You misunderstand me, Father," he said in a low voice. "Brittany Snowden is not here in the palace. She is flying back to America even as we speak."

The king frowned. "Then who is here?"

"Daphne."

"Your former—"

Murat cut him off with a quick, "Yes."

One of the many advantages of being the crown prince was the ability to assert his will on others. Ten years ago, when his former fiancée had left without so much as a note, he'd forbidden any to speak her name. All had obeyed except his father, who did not need to pay attention to the will of the crown prince.

"She attempts to defy me," Murat said as he walked to the window and leaned against the sill. "She stood there and told me she would not permit me to marry her niece." He laughed harshly. "As if her desires matter at all to me. I am Crown Prince Murat of Bahania. I determine my fate. No one, especially not a mere woman, dares to instruct me."

His father nodded. "I see. So you complain that Daphne wants to prevent you from marrying someone whom you did not want to marry in the first place."

"That is not the point," Murat told him as he folded

his arms across his chest. "There is a principle at stake. The woman did not respect my position ten years ago and nothing has changed."

"I can see how that would be difficult," the king said. "Where is she now?"

Murat glanced down as one of his father's cats stood on the sofa, stretched, then curled back up and closed its eyes.

"I have offered her a place to stay while this is sorted out," he said.

"I'm surprised Daphne would want to remain in the palace. She has delivered her message."

Murat stared at his father. "I did not give her a choice. I had the guards deliver her to the harem."

Very little startled the king, so Murat enjoyed seeing his father's mouth drop open with surprise.

"The harem?" the older man repeated.

Murat shrugged. "I had to detain her. Although she has defied me and spoken with disrespect, I was not willing to lock her in the dungeons. The harem is pleasant enough and will hold her until I decide I wish to let her go."

Although that section of the palace hadn't been used for its intended purpose for more than sixty years, the rooms themselves were maintained in their original splendor. Daphne would be surrounded by every luxury, except that of her freedom.

"It is her own fault," he added. "She had no right to interfere and keep her niece from me. Even though I was never interested in Brittany and only agreed to meet with her to please you, Daphne was wrong to try to foil me."

"I understand completely," his father said. "What do you intend to do with her now?"

Murat hadn't done anything but react. He had no plan where she was concerned.

"I do not know," he admitted.

"Will you order the plane to return Brittany to Bahania?"

"No. I know you wanted me to consider her, but in truth, Father, I could not be less interested." While Murat accepted that he had to marry and produce heirs, he could not imagine spending the rest of his life with a foolish young wife.

"Perhaps I will keep Daphne for a few days," Murat said. "To teach her a lesson."

"In the harem?" his father asked.

"Yes." He smiled. "She will be most displeased."

She would argue and fume and call him names. She would continue to defy him. Despite all that had gone on before—what she had done and what he had yet to forgive—he found himself looking forward to the encounter.

Daphne discovered her luggage in one of the largest bedrooms in the harem. The sleeping quarters consisted of several private rooms, reserved for those in favor with the king, and large dormitory-like rooms with ten or twelve beautiful beds lined up against the thick walls.

She doubted there was any furniture newer than a hundred years old. Handmade rugs covered the tiled floors in the sleeping rooms, while carved and gilded pieces of furniture added to the decor.

She ignored the suitcases and instead walked close to the walls. No one could have come in through the main door to deliver her luggage—she would have seen. Which meant there was a secret passage and door. The getting in didn't interest her as much as the getting out.

When a careful exploration of the rough walls didn't reveal any hidden doorway, she moved to the hall. It had to be somewhere. She felt around furniture and baseboards, paying particular attention to the inner walls. Still she found nothing.

"I'm sure I'll have plenty of time to keeping checking," she said aloud as she paused in front of a French door that led to a massive walled garden.

Daphne stepped out into the late-afternoon sun and breathed in the scent of the lush plant life. There were trees and shrubs, tiny flowers and huge birds of paradise. A narrow path led through the garden, while stone benches offered a place to sit and reflect. Fluttering movement caught her attention, and she glanced up in time to see two parrots fly across the open area.

"Their loud cries cover the sound of women's voices."

Daphne spun toward the speaker and saw Murat standing behind her. He still wore his suit and his imperious expression. She hated that he was the most handsome man she'd ever met and that, instead of being furious, she actually felt a little tingle of pleasure at seeing him.

Betrayed by her hormones, she thought in disgust. While leaving him ten years ago had been completely sensible, it had taken her far too long to stop loving him. Even the pain of knowing he hadn't cared enough to come after her hadn't made the recovery any shorter.

"Many of the parrots here are quite old," he continued. "But there is a single breeding pair that has given us a new generation."

"You no longer have women in the harem. Why do you keep the parrots?"

He shrugged. "Sometimes there is difficulty in letting go of the old ways. But you are not interested in our traditions. You wish to berate me and tell me what I can and cannot do." He nodded. "You may begin now if you wish."

Suspicious of his motives, she studied him. But his dark eyes and chiseled features gave nothing away. Still, that didn't stop her from wanting to know what was going to happen.

"What are you going to do about Brittany?" she asked.

"Nothing."

Like she believed that. "Are you ordering the jet to turn around?"

"No. Despite what you think of me, I will not force my bride to present herself. She will be here in time."

Daphne glared at him. "No, she won't. Brittany isn't going to marry you."

He dismissed her with a flick of his hand. "The gardens have grown since you were last here. Do you remember? You were quite enchanted with the idea of the harem and disappointed that we no longer used it for its original purpose."

"I was not," she protested. "I think it's terrible that women were kept locked up for the sole purpose of offering sexual pleasure for the king."

He smiled. "So you say now. But I distinctly recall how you found the idea exciting. You asked endless questions."

Daphne felt heat on her cheeks. Okay, maybe she *had* been a little interested in the workings of the harem. Ten years ago she'd been all of twenty and a virtual innocent in the ways of the world. Everything about the palace had intrigued her. Especially Murat.

"I'm over it now," she said. "How long do you intend to keep me here?"

"I have not yet decided."

"My family will come to my rescue. You must know they have substantial political power."

He didn't seem the least bit intimidated by the threat.

"What I know," he said, "is that their ambitions have not changed. They still wish for a Snowden female to marry royalty."

She couldn't argue that. First her parents had pushed her at Murat, and now her own sister pushed Brittany.

"I'm not like them," she said.

"How true." He glanced at his watch. "Dinner is at seven. Please dress appropriately."

She laughed. "And if I don't want to have dinner with you?"

He raised one eyebrow. "The choice has never been yours, Daphne. When will you finally learn that? Besides, you *do* want to dine with me. You have many questions. I see them in your eyes."

With that he turned and left.

"Annoying man," she muttered when she was alone again. Worse, he was right. She had questions—lots of them. And a burning desire to deal with the unfinished business between them.

As for the man himself…time had changed him, but it had not erased *her* interest in the only man she had ever loved.

Chapter Three

Daphne stood in front of her open suitcase and stared down at the contents. While a part of her wanted to ignore Murat's demand that she "dress appropriately" for their dinner, another part of her liked the idea of looking so fabulous that she would leave him speechless. It was a battle between principles and beauty and she already knew which would win.

After sorting through the contents of her luggage, she withdrew a simple sleeveless dress and carried it into the bathroom. She would let it hang in the steam while she showered. She plugged in the electric curlers she'd already unpacked, then pinned up her hair and stepped into the shower.

Fifteen minutes later she emerged all cleaned and buffed and smoothed. The bath towels provided were big enough to carpet an entire room. An array of cosmetics and skin-care products filled the cabinets by the huge mirror and vanity.

Everywhere she looked she saw marble, gold, carved wood or beveled glass. How many women had stood in front of this mirror and prepared to meet a member of the royal family? What kind of stories had these walls witnessed? How much laughter? How many tears? Under other circumstances she could enjoy her stay in this historical part of the palace.

"Who am I kidding?" she murmured as she unpinned her hair and brushed it out. "I'm enjoying it now."

She'd always loved Bahania and the palace. Murat had been the problem.

He hadn't been that way in the beginning. He'd been charming and intriguing and exactly the kind of man she'd always wanted to meet. As she reached for the first hot curler, she remembered that party she'd attended in Spain where they had first met.

Traveling through Europe the summer between her sophomore and junior year of college had meant doing her best to avoid all her parents' upper-class and political friends. But in Barcelona, Daphne had finally caved to her mother's insistence that she accept an invitation to a cocktail party for some ambassador or prime minister or something. She'd been bored and ready to leave after ten minutes. But then, on a stone balcony with a perfect view of the sunset, she'd met a man.

He'd been tall, handsome and he'd made her laugh when he'd confessed that he needed her help—that he was hiding from the far-too-amorous youngest daughter of their host.

"When she comes upstairs looking for me, I'll hide under the table and you will send her away," he said. "Will you do that for me?"

He stared at her with eyes as dark as midnight. At that second her stomach had flipped over, her cheeks had flushed and she would have followed him to the ends of the earth.

He'd spent the entire evening with her, escorting her to dinner and then dancing with her under the stars. They'd talked of books and movies, of childhood fantasies and grown-up dreams. And when he'd walked her back to her hotel and kissed her, she'd known that she was in danger of falling for him.

He hadn't told her who he was until their third date. At first she'd been nervous—after all, even she had never met a prince—but then she realized that for once being a Snowden was a good thing. She'd been raised to be the wife of a president, or even a prince.

"Come back with me," he'd pleaded when he had to return to Bahania. "Come see my country, meet my people. Let them discover how delightful you are, as I have."

It wasn't a declaration of love—she saw that now. But at twenty, it had been enough. She'd abandoned the rest of her tour and had flown with him to Bahania, where she'd stayed at the fabled Pink Palace and had fallen deeply in love with both Murat and every part of his world.

Daphne finished applying her makeup, then unwrapped the towel and stepped into her lingerie. Next she took out the curlers and carefully finger-combed her hair before bending over and spraying the underside. She flipped her hair back and applied more hairspray before finally stepping into her dress.

The silk skimmed over her body to fall just above her knees. She stepped into high-heeled sandals, then stared at her reflection.

Daphne knew she looked tired. No doubt her mother could find several items to criticize. But what would Murat think? How was the woman different from the girl? Ten years ago she'd loved him with a devotion that had bordered on mindlessness. The only thing that could have forced her to leave was the one thing that had— the realization that he didn't love her back.

"Don't go there," she told herself as she turned away from the mirror and made her way out of the bathroom.

Maybe if she arrived at the main rooms early, she could see where the secret door was as the staff arrived with dinner. She had a feeling that Murat would not be letting her out of the harem anytime soon—certainly not for meals. Which meant meals would have to come to her.

But as she stepped into the large salon overlooking the gardens, she saw she was too late. A small cart with drinks stood in the center of the room, but even more interesting than that was the man waiting by the French doors.

She'd been thinking about him while getting ready, so seeing him now made her feel as if she'd stepped into an alternative universe—one where she could summon handsome princes at will.

He turned toward her and smiled.

"You are early," he said.

"I'd hoped to catch the staff delivering dinner."

One dark eyebrow rose. "I fail to see the excitement of watching them come in and out of the door."

"You're right. If they're using the door, it's not exciting at all. But if they were to use the secret passage…"

His smile widened. "Ah. You seek to escape. But it will not be so easy. You forget we have a tradition of holding beautiful women captive. If they were able to find their way from the palace, we would be thought of as fools."

"Is that your way of saying you'll make sure I don't find the secret passage?"

He walked toward the drinks cart. "No. It is my way of saying that it is impossible to open the door from this side. Only someone outside the harem can work the latch."

He held up a bottle of champagne and she nodded.

"I suppose that information shouldn't surprise me," she told him. "So there really is no escape?"

"Why would you want there to be?"

He popped the bottle expertly, then poured two glasses.

"I don't take well to being someone's prisoner," she said as she took the glass he offered.

"But this is paradise."

"Want to trade?"

Amusement brightened his eyes. "I see you have not changed. Ten years ago you spoke your mind and you still do today."

"You mean I haven't learned my place?"

"Exactly."

"I like to think my place is wherever I want it to be."

"How like a woman." He held up his glass. "A toast to our mutual past, and what the future will bring."

She thought about Brittany, who would be landing in New York shortly. "How about to our separate lives?"

"Not so very separate. We could be family soon."

"I don't think so. You're not marrying—"

"To the beauty of the Snowden women," he said, cutting her off. "Come, Daphne. Drink with me. We will leave our discussion of less pleasant matters to another day."

"Fine." The longer they talked about other things, the more time her niece had to get safely home. "To Bahania."

"At last something we can agree upon."

They touched glasses, then sipped their champagne. Murat motioned to one of the large sofas and waited until she was seated before joining her on the overstuffed furniture.

"You are comfortable here?" he asked.

"Aside from the whole idea of being kept against my will, pretty much." She set down the glass and sighed. "Okay. Honestly, the harem is beautiful. I plan to do some serious exploring while I'm here."

"My sister, Sabrina, is an expert on antiquities and our history. Would you like me to have her visit?"

Daphne laughed. "My own private lecture circuit? I'm sure your sister has better things to do with her life."

"Than serve me?"

He spoke teasingly, but she knew there was truth behind the humor. Murat had been raised to believe he was the center of the universe. She supposed that came with being the future king.

He sat angled toward her, his hand-tailored suit emphasizing the strength in his powerful body. Ten years ago he'd been the most handsome man she'd ever met. And now... She sighed. Not that much had changed.

"Did you get a chance to see much of the city as you drove in?" he asked.

"Just the view from the highway. I was pretty intent on getting to the palace."

"Ah, yes. So you could defy me at every turn. There are many new buildings in our financial district."

"I noticed those. The city is growing."

He nodded. "We seek success in the future without losing what is precious to us from our past. It is an act of balance."

She picked up her glass of champagne and took a sip. The cool, bubbly liquid tickled her tongue. "There have been other changes since I was last here," she said. "Your brothers have married."

"That is true. All to American women. There have been many editorials in the papers about why that is, although the consensus among the people is new blood will improve the lineage of the royal family."

"That must make the women in question feel really special."

He leaned back against the sofa. "Why would they not be pleased to improve the gene pool of such a noble family?"

"Few women fantasize about being a good brood mare."

He shook his head. "Why do you always want to twist things around to make me look bad? All my sisters-in-law are delightful women who are blissfully happy with their chosen mates. Cleo and Emma have given birth in the past year. Billie is newly pregnant. They are catered to by devoted husbands and do not want for anything."

He painted a picture that made her feel funny inside. Not sad, exactly. Just…envious. She'd always wanted a guy who would love her with his whole heart, but somehow she'd never seemed to find him.

"You're right," she said. "Everyone seems perfectly happy. You remain the last single prince."

He grimaced. "A point pressed home to me on a daily basis."

"Getting a little pressure to marry and produce heirs?"

"You have no idea."

"Then we should talk about Brittany and why that would never work."

His gaze lingered on her face. "You are a difficult and stubborn woman."

"So you keep saying."

"We will discuss your niece when I decide it is time."

"You don't get to choose," she told him.

"Of course I do. And you do not wish to speak of her right now. You wish to tell me all about yourself. What you have been doing since we last met. You want to impress me."

"I do not."

He raised one eyebrow and waited. She shifted in her seat. Okay, yes, maybe she wouldn't mind knocking his socks off with her accomplishments, but she didn't like that he'd guessed.

"Come, Daphne," he said, moving closer and focusing all of his considerable attention on her. "Tell me everything. Did you finish college? What have you been doing?" He picked up her left hand and examined the bare fingers. "I see you have not given your heart to anyone."

She didn't like the assessment, nor did she appreciate the tingles that rippled up from her hand to her arm. He'd always been able to do that—reduce her to pudding with a single touch. Why couldn't that have changed? Why couldn't time away have made her immune?

"I'm not engaged, if that's what you mean," she said. "I'm not willing to discuss the state of my heart with you. It's none of your business."

"As you wish. Tell me about college."

She clutched her champagne in her right hand and thought about swallowing the whole thing in one big gulp. It might provide her with a false sense of courage, which was better than no courage at all.

"I completed my degree as planned, then went on to become a veterinarian."

He looked two parts delighted, one part surprised. "Good for you. You enjoy the work?"

"Very much. Until recently I've been with a large practice in Chicago. My first two years with them I spent summers in Indiana, working on a dairy farm."

She couldn't remember ever really shocking Murat before, so now she allowed herself to enjoy his expression of astonishment. "Delivering calves?"

"Pretty much."

"It is not seemly."

She laughed. "It was my job. I loved it. But lately I've been working with small animals. Dogs, cats, birds. The usual." She took another sip and smiled. "If your father needs any help with the cats he should let me know."

"I will be sure to pass along your offer. Chicago is very different from Bahania."

"I agree. For one thing, there aren't any words to describe how cold that wind can be in the winter."

"We have no such discomfort here."

That was true. The weather in paradise was pretty darned good.

"You're not very close to your family," he said.

Daphne nearly spilled her champagne. Okay, so it didn't take a rocket scientist to figure out that she didn't fit in with the "real" Snowdens, but she was surprised Murat would say something like that so blatantly. After all…

The light went on in her head. "You mean I live far away," she said.

"Yes. They are all on the East Coast. Is that the reason you chose to settle in Chicago?"

"Part of it," she admitted. "I handle the constant disapproval better from a distance."

"Aren't your parents proud of what you have accomplished?"

"Not really. They keep waiting for me to wake up and get engaged to a senator. I'm resisting the impulse."

She spoke with a casualness, as if her family's expectations didn't matter, but Murat saw the truth in her blue eyes.

Pain, he thought. Pain from disappointing them, pain from not being accepted for who and what she was. Daphne had always been stubborn and determined and proud. From what he could see, little had changed about that.

Her appearance had been altered, though. Her face was thinner, her features more defined. Whereas at twenty she had held the promise of great beauty, now she fulfilled it. There was an air of confidence about her he liked.

She leaned forward. "I've spent the past couple of years studying pet psychology."

"I have not heard of that."

She smiled again, her full lips curving upward as if she were about to share a delicious private joke. "You'd appreciate it. The field is growing rapidly. We're interested in why animals act the way they do. What set of circumstances combine with their personality to make them act aggressively or chew furniture or not accept a new baby. That sort of thing."

He couldn't believe such information existed. "This is what you are doing now?"

"I'm getting into it. I've learned some interesting things about dealing with alpha males." She tilted her head. "Maybe I could use the techniques to tame you."

"Neither of us is interested in me being tame."

"Oh, I don't know."

"I do."

"You're certainly sure of yourself."

"The privilege of being the alpha male."

She continued to study him. Awareness crackled between them. He could smell the faint scent of the soap she'd used and some other subtle fragrance he associated only with her.

Wanting coiled low in his gut, surprising him with both its presence and its intensity. After all this time? He'd always wondered what he would feel if he saw her again, but somehow he'd never expected to have a strong need to touch her, explore her, take her.

He wanted to lead her into one of the many harem bedrooms and make her shudder beneath him. Funny how so much time had passed and the desire hadn't gone away.

"You're looking very predatory," she said. "What are you thinking?"

"I was wondering about your art. Do you still make time to do your sculptures?"

She hesitated, as if she didn't quite believe that was what he'd been thinking, then she answered.

"I still love it, but time is always an issue."

"Perhaps I should provide you with clay while you are here. You can indulge your passion."

"How long do you intend to keep me in the harem?"

"I have not yet decided."

"So we really do need to talk about Brittany."

Just then the large golden doors opened and several servants walked in pushing carts.

"Dinner," he said, rising to his feet.

"If I didn't know better, I would say you did that on purpose."

He smiled. "Even I can't command my staff with just a thought."

"Why do I know you're working on it?"

"I have no idea."

Murat had left the menu up to his head chef, and he was not disappointed with the meal. Neither was Daphne, he thought as she ran her fork across the remaining crumbs of chocolate from the torte served for dessert.

"Amazing," she breathed. "I could blow up like a beached whale if I lived here for too long."

"Not every meal is so very formal," he said, enjoying her pleasure in the food.

"Good thing. I'll have to do about fifty laps in the garden tomorrow." She picked up her wine and eyed him over the glass. "Unless you plan on cutting me loose sometime soon."

"Are we back to that?"

"We are. Murat, I'm serious. You can't keep me here forever."

"Perhaps I wish to resume the traditional use of these rooms."

He held in a smile as her eyes widened. "You are *so* kidding," she said, although she didn't sound quite sure of herself. "I'm not going to volunteer."

"Few women did at first, even though it was a great honor. But in time they came to enjoy their lives. Luxury, pleasure. What more could you want?"

"How about freedom and autonomy?"

"There is power in being desired. The smart women learned that and used it to their advantage. They ruled the ruler."

"I've never been good at subterfuge," she told him. "Besides, I'm not interested in working behind the scenes. I want to be up front and in the thick of things. I want to be an equal."

"That will never be. I am to be king of Bahania, with all the advantages and disadvantages that go with the position."

Daphne sipped her dessert wine. Disadvantages? She hadn't thought there could be any. Even if there weren't, it was a much safer topic than what life would be like in the harem.

"What's so bad about being the king?" she asked.

"Nothing bad, as you say. Just restrictions. Rules. Responsibilities."

"Always being in the spotlight," she said. "Always having to do the right thing."

"Exactly."

"Marrying a teenager you've never met can't be right, Murat, can it?"

His gaze narrowed. "You are persistent."

"And determined. I love her. I would do anything for her."

"Even displease me?"

"Apparently," she said with a shrug. "Are you going to behead me for it?"

"Your casual question tells me you are not in the least bit worried. I will have to do something to convince you of my power."

"I'm very clear on your power. I just want you to use it for good." She set down her glass and leaned toward him. "Come on. It's just the two of us, and I promise never to tell. You can't have been serious about her. A young girl you've never met?"

"Perhaps I wanted a brainless young woman to do my bidding."

Daphne stiffened. "She's not brainless. And she wouldn't have done your bidding. You're trying to annoy me on purpose, aren't you?"

"Is it working?"

"Pretty much." She sagged back in her chair. "I don't want you to be like that. I don't want you to be the kind of man who would marry Brittany."

"Do you think I am?"

"I hope not. But even if you are, I won't let you."

"You can't stop me."

"I'll do whatever is necessary to stop you."

His dark eyes twinkled with amusement. "I am Crown Prince Murat of Bahania. Who are you to threaten me?"

Good question. Maybe it was the night and the man, or just the alcohol, but her head was a little fuzzy. There had been a different wine with each course. She'd only taken a sip of each, but those sips added up and muddled her thinking. It was the only explanation for what she said next.

"You're just some alpha-male dog peeing on every tree to mark his territory. That's all Brittany is to you. A tree or a bush."

As soon as the words were out, she wanted to call them back. Murat stunned her by tossing back his head and roaring with laughter.

Still chuckling, he stood. "Come, we will go for a walk to clear your head. You can tell me all your theories about domesticating men such as me."

He walked around the table and pulled back her chair. She rose and faced him.

"It's not a joke. You're acting like a territorial German shepherd. You could use a little obedience training to keep you in line."

"I am not the one who needs to stay in line."

"Are you threatening me?"

As she spoke, she took a step toward him. Unfortunately her feet weren't getting the right signals from her brain, and she stumbled. He caught her and pulled her against him.

"You speak of domestication, but is that what you want?" he asked. "A trained man would not do this."

The "this" turned out to be nothing more than his mouth pressing against hers. A kiss. No biggie.

Except the second his lips brushed against hers, every part of her body seemed to go up in flames. Desperate hot need pulsed through her, forcing her to cling to him or collapse at his feet.

They kissed before, she remembered hazily. A lifetime ago. He'd held her tenderly and delighted her with gentle embraces.

But not this time. Now he claimed her with a passion that left her breathless and hungry for more. He wrapped his arms around her, drawing her up against his hard body.

She melted into him, savoring the heat and the strength. When he tilted his head, she did the same and parted her lips before he even asked. He plunged inside, stroking, circling, teasing, making her breath catch and her body weep with desire.

More, she thought as she kissed him back. There had to be more.

But there wasn't. He straightened, forcing her to consider standing on her own. She pushed back and found her balance, then struggled to catch her breath.

"Brittany will be in New York by now," he said.

The sudden change in topic caught her off guard. Weren't they going to discuss the kiss? Weren't they going to do it again?

Apparently not. She ordered herself to focus on Brittany. Murat. The wedding that could never be.

"I meant what I said," he told her. "There *will* be a Snowden bride."

"You'll need to rethink your plan," she said. "Brittany isn't going to marry you."

He stared at her, his dark eyes unreadable. "Are you sure?"

"Absolutely."

She braced herself for an argument or at least a pronouncement that he was the crown prince, blah, blah, blah. Instead he simply nodded.

"As you wish," he said. And then he left.

Daphne didn't fall asleep until sometime after two in the morning. She'd felt too out of sorts to relax. While she told herself she should be happy that Murat was finally seeing reason about Brittany, she didn't trust the man. Certainly not his last cryptic agreement. As she wished what? Was he really giving up on Brittany so easily? Somehow that didn't seem right.

So when she woke early the next morning, she felt more tired than when she'd gone to bed.

After slipping into her robe, she hurried toward the smell of fresh coffee wafting through the harem. A cart stood by the sofa.

Daphne ignored the fresh fruit and croissants and dove for the coffee. The steaming liquid perked her up with the first sip.

"Better," she said, when she'd swallowed half a cup.

She sat down in front of the cart and picked up the

folded newspapers. The first was a copy of *USA TODAY*. Underneath was the local Bahanian paper. She flipped it open, then screamed.

On the front page was a color picture of her under a headline announcing her engagement to Murat.

Chapter Four

"I'll kill him!" Daphne yelled.

She set down her coffee before she dropped it and shrieked her fury.

"How dare he? Who does he think he is? Crown prince or not, I'll have his head for this!"

She couldn't believe it. Last night he'd been friendly and fun and sexy with his talking and touching, when the whole time he'd been planning an ambush.

She stomped her foot. He'd *kissed* her. He'd taken her in his arms and kissed her. She'd gotten all gooey and nostalgic while he'd known what he was going to do.

"Bastard. No. Wait. He's lower than that. He's a…a camel-dung sweeper. He's slime."

She tossed the paper down, then immediately bent over to pick it up. There, in perfect English, was the announcement for the upcoming wedding along with what looked like a very long story on her previous engagement to Murat.

"Just great," she muttered. "Now we're going to have to rehash that again."

She threw the paper in the air and stalked around the room. "Are you listening, Murat?" she yelled. "Because if you are, know that you've gone too far. You can't do this to me. I won't let you."

There was no answer. Typical, she thought. He's done it and now he was hiding out.

Just then the phone rang.

"Ha! Afraid to face me in person?"

She crossed to the phone on the end table and snatched it up. "Yes?"

"How could you do this?" a familiar female voice demanded.

"Laurel?"

A choke shook her sister's voice. "Who else? Dammit, Daphne, you always have to ruin everything. You did this on purpose, didn't you? You wanted him for yourself."

It took Daphne a second to figure out what her sister was talking about. "You know about the engagement?" she asked.

"Of course. What did you think? That it would happen in secret?"

"Of course not. I mean there's no engagement."

How on earth had her sister found out? There was a major time difference between Bahania and the American East Coast. "Shouldn't you be in bed?"

"Oh, sure. Because I'm going to sleep after this." Her sister drew in a ragged breath. "What I don't understand is how you could do this to Brittany. I thought you really cared about her."

"I do. I love her." Probably more than her sister ever had, Daphne thought grimly. "That's why I didn't want her marrying Murat. She's never even met the man."

"You took care of things, didn't you? Now you have him all for yourself. I can't believe I was stabbed in the back by my own sister."

Daphne clutched the phone. "This is crazy. Laurel, think about it. Why on earth would I want to marry Murat? Didn't I already dump him once?"

"You've probably regretted it ever since. You've just been waiting for the right opportunity to pounce."

"It's been ten years. Couldn't I have pounced before now?"

"You thought you'd find someone else. But you didn't. Who could measure up to the man who's going to be king? I understand that kind of ambition. I can even respect it. But to steal your only niece's fiancé is horrible. Brittany will be crushed."

"I doubt that."

"I never should have trusted you," Laurel said. "Why didn't I see what you had planned?"

"There wasn't a plan." Except making sure Brittany didn't throw her life away, but Laurel didn't have to know about that. "I told you, I'm not engaged to Murat. I don't know what the papers are talking about, but it's a huge mistake."

"Oh, sure. Like I believe that."

"Believe what you want. There's not going to be a wedding."

"Tell that to my heartsick daughter. You've always thought of yourself instead of your family. Just know I'll never forgive you. No matter what."

With that, Laurel hung up.

Daphne listened to the silence for a second, then put down the phone and covered her face with her hands. Nothing made sense. How could this be happening?

She had a lot of questions, but no answers, and she knew only one way to get them.

She stood and crossed to the heavy gold doors.

"Hey," she yelled. "Are you guards still out there?"

"Yes, ma'am. Is there a problem?"

"You bet there is. Tell Murat I want to see him right now."

She heard low conversation but not the individual words as the guards spoke to each other.

"We'll pass your message along to the crown prince," one of the men said at last.

"Not good enough. I want his royal fanny down here this second. And you can tell him I said that."

She pounded on the door a couple of times for good measure, then stalked back into her bedroom. Suddenly the phrase "dressed to kill" took on a whole new meaning.

* * *

Murat finished his second cup of coffee as he read over the financial section of the *London Times*. Then the door to his suite opened, and his father stepped in.

The king was perfectly dressed, even with the Persian cat he carried in his arms. He nodded at the guard on duty, then walked into the dining room.

"Good morning," he said.

Murat rose and motioned to a chair. The king shook his head.

"I won't be staying long. I only came by to discuss the most fascinating item I saw in the paper this morning."

"That the value of the Euro is expected to rise?" Murat asked calmly, knowing it wasn't that.

"No." The king flipped through the pages until he found the local edition—the one with the large picture of Daphne on the front page. "Interesting solution."

Murat shrugged. "I said I would have a Snowden bride, and so I shall."

"I'm surprised she agreed."

Murat thought of the message he'd received from the guards outside the harem. Even though he suspected they'd edited the content, Daphne's demands made him smile.

"She has not," he admitted. "But she will. After all, the choice of fiancées was hers alone."

"Oh?"

"I told her there would be a wedding, and she said Brittany would not be the bride. That left Daphne to fill the position."

"I see." His father didn't react at all. "Do you have a time line in place for this wedding?"

"Four months."

"Not long to prepare for such an important occasion."

"I think we will manage."

"Perhaps I should go to her and offer my congratulations."

Murat raised his eyebrows. "I'm sure Daphne will welcome your visit, but may I suggest you wait a few days. Until she has had time to settle in to the idea of being my wife."

"Perhaps you are right." The king stroked the cat in his arms. "You have chosen wisely."

"Thank you. I'm sure Daphne and I will be very happy together." After she got over wanting him dead.

By ten that morning Daphne was convinced she'd worn a track in the marble tile floors. She'd showered, dressed and paced. So far she'd been unable to make any phone calls because of the stupid time difference. But she would eventually get through to someone and then Murat would taste her fury. She might not be the favorite Snowden, but she was still a member of the family and her name meant something. She would call in every favor possible and make him pay for this.

"Of all the arrogant, insensitive, chauvinistic, ridiculous ideas," she muttered as she walked to the French doors.

"So much energy."

She spun and saw him moving toward her. "I hate

that you do that," she said. "Appear and disappear. I swear, when I find that secret door, I'm putting something in front of it so you can't use it anymore."

He seemed completely unruffled by her anger. "As you wish."

"Oh, sure. You say that now. Where were my wishes last night when you were sending your lies to the newspaper?" She stalked over to the dining room table and picked up the pages in question.

"How could you do this?" she asked as she shook them at him. "How dare you? Who gave you the right?"

"You did."

"What?" She hated that she practically shrieked, but the man was making her insane. "I most certainly did not."

"I told you there would be a Snowden bride and you declared it would not be your niece."

"What?" she repeated. "That's not making a choice. I never agreed with your original premise. Where do you get off saying you'll have a Snowden bride? We're not ice cream flavors to be ordered interchangeably. We're people."

"Yes, I know. Women. I have agreed not to marry Brittany. You should be pleased."

Pleased? "Are you crazy?" She dropped the papers and clutched at the back of the chair. "I'm furious. You've trapped me here and told lies about me to the press. I've already heard from my sister. Do you know how this is going to mess up my life? Both of our lives?"

"I agree that marriage will change things, but I'm hoping for the better."

"We're not getting married!" she yelled.

Instead of answering, he simply stared at her. Calm certainty radiated from him in nearly palpable waves. It made her want to choke him.

She drew in a deep breath and tried to relax. When that didn't work, she attempted to loosen her grip on the chair.

"Okay," she said. "Let's start from the beginning. You're not marrying Brittany, which is a good thing."

He had the gall to smile at her. "Did you really think I would be interested in a teenager for my wife? Bringing Brittany here was entirely my father's idea. I agreed to meet with her only to make him happy."

Spots appeared before her eyes. "You what?" No way. That couldn't be true. "Tell me that again."

"I never intended to marry Brittany."

"But you…" She couldn't breathe. Her chest felt hot and tight and she couldn't think. "But you said…"

"I wanted to annoy you for assuming the worst about me. Then when you offered yourself in Brittany's place, I decided to consider the possibility."

Offer? "I never offered."

"Oh, but you did. And I accepted."

"No. You can't." She pulled out the chair and sank onto the seat. "I know you're used to getting your way, but this time it isn't going to happen. I need to be very clear about that. There isn't going to be a wedding. You can't make me, and if you try, you'll be forced to tie me up and gag me as you drag me down the aisle. Won't that play well in the press."

"I do not care about the press."

She grabbed the paper again. "Then why did you bother telling them this?"

He sat down across from her. "Make no mistake. My mind is made up. We *will* be married. This announcement has forced you to see the truth. Now you will have time to accept it."

"What I accept is that you've slipped into madness. This isn't the fifteenth century. You can't force me to do what you want. This is a free country." She remembered she wasn't in America anymore. "Sort of."

"I am Crown Prince Murat of Bahania. Few would tell me no."

"Count me among them."

He leaned back in his chair. "You never disappoint me," he said. "How I enjoy the explosion. You're like fireworks."

She glared at him. "You haven't seen anything yet. I'll take this all the way to the White House if I have to."

"Good. The president will be invited to the wedding. He and I have been friends for many years now."

At that moment Daphne desperately wished for superpowers so she could overturn the heavy table and toss Murat out the window.

"I'm going to speak slowly," she said. "So you can understand me. I…won't…marry…you. I have a life. Friends. My work."

"Ah, yes. About your work. I made some phone calls last night and found it most interesting to learn that you have left your veterinary practice in Chicago."

"That was about making career choices, not marrying you."

"And you have been very determined to keep me from your niece. Are you sure you do not secretly want me for yourself?"

She rolled her eyes. "How amazing that you and your ego fit inside the room at the same time." Although her sister had made the same accusation.

It wasn't true, Daphne reminded herself. Murat was her past, and she was more than content to keep him there. She hadn't spent the last ten years pining. She'd dated, been happy. He was a non-event.

"I haven't thought about you in ages," she said honestly. "I'm even willing to take an oath. Just bring in the Bible. I wouldn't be here now if you hadn't acted all caveman over my niece. This is your fault."

He nodded. "There is a ring."

She blinked at him. "What? You want to try to buy me off with jewelry? Thank you very much but I'm not that kind of woman."

He smiled again. "I know."

Her rage returned, but before she could decide how to channel it, the phone rang again.

She hesitated before crossing the room to answer it. Was Laurel calling back to yell some more? Daphne had a feeling she was at the end of her rope and not up to taking that particular call. But what if it was Brittany, and her niece really was upset?

"Not possible," she said as she crossed to the phone and picked it up. "This is Daphne."

"Darling, we just heard. We're delighted."

Her mother's voice came over the line as clearly as if she'd been in the same room.

Daphne clutched the receiver. "Laurel called?"

"Yes. Oh, darling, how clever you are to have finally snagged Murat. The man who will be king." Her mother sighed. "I always knew you'd do us proud."

Daphne didn't know what to think. She wanted to tell her mother the truth—that there wasn't going to be a wedding, that this was all a mistake, but she couldn't seem to speak.

"Your father is simply thrilled," her mother said. "We're looking forward to a lovely wedding. Do you have any idea when?"

"I—"

Her mother laughed. "Of course you don't. You've only just become engaged. Well, let me know as soon as the date is finalized. We'll need to rearrange some travel, but it will be worth it. Your father can't wait to walk you down the aisle."

Daphne turned her back so Murat couldn't see her expression. She didn't want him to know how much this conversation hurt.

"Laurel was pretty upset," she said, not knowing what else to say.

"I know. She got it in her head that Brittany would be the one for Murat. Honestly, the girl is lovely and will make a fine marriage in time, but she's just too young. There are responsibilities that come with being queen, and she simply wasn't ready." Her mother laughed.

"Queen. I like the sound of that. My daughter, the queen. My sweet baby girl. All right, I'm going to run, but I'll call soon. You must be so very happy. This is wonderful, Daphne. Truly wonderful."

With that her mother hung up. Daphne replaced the receiver and did her best not to react in any way. Sure, her eyes burned and her body felt tense and sore, but she would get over it. She always did.

"Your parents?" Murat asked from his place at the table behind her.

She nodded. "My mother. My sister called and spoke with her. She's d-delighted."

The crack in her voice made her stiffen. No way was she going to give in to the emotion pulsing through her.

"She wants details about the wedding as soon as possible. So she can rearrange their travel schedule."

"You did not tell her there wouldn't be a wedding."

"No."

Because it had been too hard to speak. Because if she tried, she would give in to the pain and once that dam broke, there was no putting it together.

"Don't think that means I've accepted the engagement," she whispered.

"Not for a second."

She heard footsteps, then Murat's hands clasped her arms and he turned her toward him. Understanding darkened his eyes.

She was so unused to seeing any readable emotion in his gaze that she couldn't seem to react. Which meant she didn't protest when he pulled her close and wrapped his arms around her. Suddenly she was pressing against him, her head on his shoulder and the protective warmth of his body surrounding her.

"You can't do this," she said, her voice muffled against his suit jacket. "I hate you."

"I know you do, but right now there isn't anyone else." He stroked her hair. "Come now. Tell me what troubles you."

She shook her head. To speak of it would hurt too much.

"It's your mother," he murmured. "She said she was happy about the engagement. Your family has always been ambitious. In some ways a king for a son-in-law is even better than a president."

"I know." She wrapped her arms around his waist and hung on as hard as she could. "It's horrible. *She's* horrible. She said she was proud of me. That's the first time she's ever said that. Because I've always been a disappointment."

The hurt of a decade of indifference from her family swept through her. "Nobody came to my college graduation. Did you know that? They were all still angry because I'd refused to marry you. And they hated that I became a vet. No one even acknowledged my finishing school and going to work. My mother didn't say a word in the Christmas newsletter. She didn't mention me at all. It's as if by not marrying well, I'd ceased to exist."

She felt the light brush of his lips on her head. "I am sorry."

She sniffed. "I'm only their child when I do what

they want. I was afraid it would be the same for Brittany. I wanted her to be happy and strong so I tried to let her know that I loved her no matter what. That my love wasn't conditional on her marrying the right man."

"I'm sure she knows how much you care."

"I hope so. Laurel said she would be heartbroken."

Murat chuckled. "Not to marry a man twice her age whom she has never met? I suspect you raised her better than that."

"What?" She lifted her head and stared at him. They were far closer than she'd realized, which was really stupid—what with her being in his arms and all.

"I didn't raise her," she said. "She's not my daughter."

"Isn't she?"

It was what she'd always believed in her heart but never spoken of. Not to anyone. How could Murat grasp that personal truth so easily?

"I know all about expectations," he said, lightly tracing the curve of her cheek. "There was not a single day I was allowed to forget my responsibilities."

Which made sense. "I guess when you're going to grow up and be king, you aren't supposed to make as many mistakes as the rest of us."

"Exactly. So I understand about having to do what others want, even when that means not doing what is in your heart."

"Except I wasn't willing to do that," she reminded him. "I did what I wanted and they punished me. Not just my parents, but my sisters, too. I ceased to exist."

His dark gaze held her captive. She liked being held

by him, which was crazy, because he was the enemy. Only, right this second, he didn't seem so bad.

"You exist to me," he said.

If only that were true. Reluctantly she pushed away and stood on her own.

"I don't," she said. "I have no idea what your engagement game is about, but I know it's not about me."

"How can you say that? You're the one I've chosen."

"Why?" she asked. "I think you're being stubborn and difficult. You don't care about me. You never did."

He frowned. "How can you say that? Ten years ago I asked you to marry me."

"What does that have to do with anything? If you'd really loved me, you wouldn't have let me go. But you didn't care when I left. I walked away and you never once came after me to find out why."

Chapter Five

Murat left Daphne and returned to his office. But despite the meeting he was supposed to attend, he told his assistant not to bother him and closed his door.

The space was large and open, as befitted the crown prince of such a wealthy nation. The conversation area of three sofas sat by several tall windows and the conference table easily seated sixteen.

Murat ignored it all as he crossed to the balcony overlooking a private garden and stepped outside. The spring air hinted at the heat to come. He ignored it and the call of the birds. Instead he stared into the distance as he wrestled with the past.

How like a woman, he thought. She questioned why

he had not gone after her when she had been the one to leave him. Why would he want to follow such a woman? Besides, even if the thought had occurred to him—which it had not—it wasn't his place. If she wished them to be in contact, then she should come crawling back, begging forgiveness for having left in the first place.

She should know all of this. She came from a family familiar with power and how the world worked. He had known that they favored the match, and he was willing to admit he had been surprised she would stand against them.

Murat turned his back on the view but did not enter his office. The past flashed before him—a tableau of what had been. His father had told him she left. The king had come to him full of plans of how they would go after her and bring her back, but Murat had refused. He would not chase her around the world. If Daphne wanted to be gone, then let her. She had been a mere woman. Easy to replace.

Now, with the wisdom of hindsight, he admitted to himself that she had been different from anyone he had ever known. As for replacing her...that had never occurred. He had met other women, bedded them, been interested and intrigued. But he had never been willing to marry any of them.

He knew he should wonder why. What was it about her that had made her stand out? Not her great beauty. She was attractive and sensual, but he had known women who seemed more goddess than human. Not her intelligence. While hers was better than average, he had dated women whose comprehension of technical and scientific matters had left him speechless.

She was funny and charming, but he had known those with more of those qualities. So what combination of traits had made him willing to marry her and not another?

As he walked back into his office, he remembered what it had been like after she had left. He hadn't allowed himself to mourn her. No one had been permitted to speak her name. For him, it was as if she had never been.

And now she had returned and they would marry. In time she would see that was right. She might always argue with him, but she knew who was in charge.

He moved to his desk and took a seat. In a locked drawer sat a red leather box that contained the official seal of his office. He opened that box and removed the seal, then moved aside the silk lining. Tucked in the bottom, in between folds of protective padding, lay a diamond ring.

The stone had been given by a Bahanian king to his favorite mistress in 1685. He had been loyal to her for nearly thirty years and when his queen died, he married his mistress. Many told the story of how the ring had saved the mistress's life more than once, as other jealous women in the harem sought to do her harm. The stone was said to possess magical powers to heal and evoke love.

Of all the diamonds in the royal family's possession, this had been the one Murat had chosen for Daphne and the one she had left behind when she'd gone. He picked it up now and studied the carefully cut stone.

Such a small thing, he thought. Barely three carats. He'd been a fool to think it contained any magic at all.

He returned the ring to its hiding place, replaced the seal, then put the box back in the drawer and locked it. Later that afternoon the royal jeweler would offer a selection of rings for Murat's consideration. He would choose another one for Daphne. A stone without history or meaning. Or magic.

Daphne spent the morning considering her options. Murat had left in a huff without saying much to make her feel any better. He refused to admit there wasn't going to be a wedding, nor had he told her how her sister and the newspaper had found out so quickly. Obviously, he was to blame, but why wouldn't he just say so?

As she walked through the garden she told herself that an unexpected engagement certainly put things in perspective. Twenty-four hours ago her biggest concern had been how long he would keep her trapped in the harem. She'd been sure he would want to make his point—that she'd defied him and had to be punished in some way—but she'd looked at it as an unexpected vacation in a place not of her choosing. Now everything was different.

She wanted to tell herself that he couldn't possibly marry her without her permission, only she didn't know if that was true. Murat was determined and obviously sneaky. Should anyone be able to pull that off—he was the guy. She was going to have to stay on her toes and prevent the wedding from happening. Finding herself married to him would be a disaster of monumental proportions. Getting out of this engagement was going to be difficult enough.

She needed a plan. Which meant she needed more information. But how to get it?

"Hello? Anybody home?"

Daphne turned toward the sound of the female voice. None of the servants would address her that way. Not after they knew about the engagement. To be honest, none of the servants had addressed her at all—it was as if they'd been told to avoid conversation.

She hurried back into the harem.

"Hello," she said as she stepped into the large, cool main room.

Three women stood together. They were beautiful, elegantly dressed and smiling.

Two blondes and a redhead. One of the blondes—a petite woman with short, spiky hair and a curvy body to die for—stepped forward.

"We're your basic princess contingent sneaking in to speak with the prisoner." She grinned. "Not that you're really a prisoner. There were rumors, of course. But now you're engaged to Murat, which makes you family. I'm Cleo. Married to Sadik." She rolled her big, blue eyes. "How totally *Lawrence of Arabia* to introduce myself in terms of who my husband is."

"You're a disgrace to us all, Cleo," the other blonde said fondly. She was a little taller, even more curvy, with big hair and sandals that looked high enough to be a walking hazard, especially considering her obvious pregnancy.

"Daphne Snowden."

"Hi." The redhead waved. "I'm Emma. Reyhan's wife." She motioned to the pregnant woman. "That's Billie."

Billie frowned. "Didn't I give her my name?"

"No," Cleo and Emma said together. Cleo sighed. "Billie thinks she's all that because she can fly jets. Like that's a big deal."

"It *is* a big deal," Emma whispered. "We talked about it."

"I know, but we don't want her to get a big head or anything."

"It'll match my big stomach," Billie said with a grin.

Daphne didn't know what to say. Just then she heard a rapid clicking sound. She glanced around and saw a small Yorkshire terrier exploring the main salon of the harem.

"That's Muffin," Billie said. "My other baby."

"I didn't know there were any dogs at the palace," Daphne said. "Doesn't the king only keep cats?"

"He's taken a liking to Muffin," Billie said. "Which is great because she gets into all kinds of trouble." She rubbed the small of her back. "Mind if I take a load off?"

"What? Oh, sorry. Please." Daphne motioned to the closest grouping of sofas. "Make yourselves comfortable."

The women sat down. Daphne stared from one to the other, not sure what to make of them. The last time she'd been in Bahania, all of Murat's brothers had been happy bachelors.

"I read about your weddings, of course," she said, then glanced at Emma. "Well, not yours."

"I know," she said as she flipped her red hair over her shoulder. "We were a scandal. But I thought the ceremony to renew our vows was very lovely."

"The pictures were great." Daphne turned to Billie. "You're married to Jefri?"

The pregnant woman nodded. "I'm embarrassed to say he swept me off my feet, and in the shoes I wear, that's a trick."

The women laughed. Daphne sensed their closeness and felt a twinge of envy. She'd never had that kind of relationship with her own sisters.

Cleo scooted forward on the sofa. "There are five of us altogether. I know it sounds confusing, but it's really simple. The king has four sons and two daughters. Of the girls, Sabrina is married to Kardal and they live, ah, out of the country. Zara, his other daughter, is married to Rafe. Zara didn't know the king was her father until a few years ago."

"I remember reading about that. Very romantic."

"I thought so," Cleo said.

Billie groaned. "You think everything is romantic."

Emma sighed. "These two argue a lot. I think they're too much alike. The fighting doesn't mean anything, but sometimes it gets a little old."

"I'm ignoring you," Cleo said to Emma.

"Me, too," Billie added.

Daphne couldn't help grinning. "Do you three live in the palace?" They could certainly make her brief stay more fun.

"*They* do," Emma said, pointing to the other two

women. "As I said, I'm married to Reyhan, and we spend much of our time out in the desert. Reyhan inherited a house there from his aunt. Billie and Jefri and Cleo and Sadik make their home in the palace. Billie and Jefri are involved with the new air force. Billie's a flight instructor. She flies jets."

Daphne couldn't imagine the big-haired sex kitten flying anything more complicated than a paper airplane. "You're kidding?"

Billie grinned. "Never underestimate the power of a woman."

"I guess not."

Emma continued. "I'm in town for a few days while Reyhan has some meetings. We brought the baby." Her face softened as she smiled. "We have a daughter."

"That's two for two," Billie said. "I have a daughter, too. Wouldn't it be funny if there weren't any male heirs?"

"Not to the men in the family," Daphne said.

"Good point," Billie said. "So Zara and Sabrina will be out in a few weeks to meet you. They said to say hi for them in the meantime."

Talk about overwhelming, Daphne thought. "You're very sweet to visit me."

"Not a problem," Cleo said. She fluffed her short, blond hair. "Besides, we want all the details. This engagement has come about very quickly."

"That's subtle," Billie said.

"Well, it has," Cleo insisted.

Emma cleared her throat. "I think what she means is

how wonderful that you and Murat have found each other."

Daphne hated to burst their bubble, but she wouldn't pretend to be something she wasn't. "Murat and I haven't found anything. I don't know why he announced we're engaged, because we're not. And there isn't going to be a wedding."

The three women looked at each other, then at her.

"That changes things," Cleo said brightly.

Daphne smoothed the hem of her skirt. "I know it sounds terrible."

"Not at all," Emma said.

"Sort of," Billie said.

Daphne couldn't help smiling. "You guys are great."

"Thanks," Cleo said, preening a little. "I like to think we're pretty special."

Daphne chuckled for a second, then sobered as she thought about her impossible situation. "My family is big into politics and power," she said. "Years ago I was traveling through Europe during a summer break from college and I met Murat. I didn't know who he was and we hit it off. When he invited me back here, I was stunned to find out I'd been dating the crown prince."

"I know that feeling," Emma said. "Reyhan isn't going to be king, but he's still royal. I had no idea."

Billie put her arm around Emma. "She's our innocent."

Daphne sighed. "Then you can imagine my shock. Before I knew what had happened, we were engaged and everything was moving so quickly."

Billie frowned. "*Were* engaged. Obviously you didn't get married."

"I think I remember reading about that," Billie said. "Ten years ago I was a serious tabloid junkie."

"You still read the tabloids," Cleo said.

"Yeah, and then you steal them from me."

"Ladies," Emma said, holding up her hand to stop their bickering. "I believe Daphne was talking."

Cleo smiled at her. "Go on, Daphne."

"There's not much else to say. Things didn't work out and I left. My family was furious and didn't speak to me for ages. Eventually we patched things up." Sort of. Her mother had never really forgiven her for not marrying a future king. "Then a few weeks ago my niece, who is barely eighteen, told me that she was flying over to meet Murat and get engaged."

Billie raised her eyebrows. "What? That doesn't sound right."

"I agree," Cleo said. "Murat can be all formal with his 'I'm the crown prince' but he's never been into silly young women." She winced. "Sorry. Not that your niece is silly or anything."

"I know what you mean," Daphne said. "She's still a kid in so many ways. She's only had a couple of boyfriends and none of them were serious. Murat is nearly twice her age. I was determined to talk her out of it, which I did, just in the nick of time. We were flying here when she suddenly realized she was making a huge mistake. So she went back to the States, and I stayed to tell Murat there wasn't going to be an engagement. The next thing I knew I was locked in the harem and he was announcing *our* engagement in the papers."

Emma sighed. "That's so romantic."

Cleo and Billie looked at her. "That's kidnapping," Cleo said.

"Well, maybe technically, but he must really love her."

Daphne shook her head. "I hate to burst your bubble, but Murat doesn't love me. It's been ten years. He doesn't even *know* me anymore."

"So why the sudden engagement?" Billie asked.

"I have no idea," Daphne told her.

"He has to have a reason," Cleo said. "Men always do things for a reason. Has he been pining for you all these years?"

"Gee, let's count the number of women he's been out with in that time," Daphne said humorously. "I'm going to guess it's around a hundred or so."

"But he wasn't serious about any of them."

Emma scooted forward in her seat. "If it's not too personal, why did you leave last time?"

Good question. "There were a lot of reasons. Things moved so quickly—I didn't get a chance to figure out if this was the life I wanted before I found myself engaged. When reality set in, I panicked."

"But you loved him," Billie said. "Didn't you?"

"As much as I could at the time." Daphne thought back to how brightly her feelings had burned. "I was pretty innocent, and Murat was the first guy I'd been serious about. I'm not sure I knew what love was. We were so different."

Although getting over him had taken what felt like a lifetime. She still had scars.

Cleo smiled at her. "Ah, to be that young again. Wouldn't you like to go back in time and talk to that Daphne?"

"I don't know what I would say to her."

"Would you tell her to stay?" Cleo asked.

"No."

"Why not?" Emma asked. "Are we getting too personal? Does this feel like an interrogation?"

"I'm okay," Daphne told her. "And I wouldn't have told her to stay because I know what happened after. Murat didn't love her…me. He didn't bother to come after me. Not a phone call or a letter. He never cared enough to find out why I'd left."

She expected the three princesses to look shocked. Instead Cleo sighed, Billie shook her head, and Emma's expression turned sad.

"It's pride," Emma said. "They have too much of it. It's a sheik thing. Or maybe a royal thing."

"I'm not sure what pride has to do with it."

Cleo shrugged. "You have to look at it from his point of view. He offered you everything, and you walked away. That had to have tweaked his tail just a little. Tweaked princes don't go running after women."

"Mere women," Billie said in a stern voice. "You are a mere woman."

Emma grinned. "The princes are so cute when they're all imperious."

Daphne felt as if she'd just sat down with the crazy family. "What are you talking about?"

"That you can't judge Murat's feelings for you solely on whether or not he came running after you when you left," Cleo said. "He's the crown prince and has that ego thing going on even more than his brothers. It's possible that in that twisted 'I'm the man' brain of his, he thought it would show too much weakness."

"But if he'd cared…"

"It's not about caring," Emma said. "You're looking at the situation logically, and like a woman. Reyhan loved me and yet he ignored me for years. His pride wouldn't let him talk to someone he thought had rejected him, let alone admit his feelings. Murat could be the same way."

Daphne thought about all the women he'd seen over the past decade. "I don't think he's actually been doing a lot of suffering."

"Maybe not," Cleo said. "But it's something to think about. If he matters at all."

Just then the gold doors opened and several servants entered with carts.

Billie smiled. "Did we mention we'd brought lunch?"

The women gathered around the dining room table and enjoyed the delicious food. Conversation shifted from Daphne and her situation to how each of them had met their husbands, then to shopping and the best place to get really gorgeous, if uncomfortable, shoes. They left a little after three.

Daphne closed the door behind them, then retreated to the sofa in front of the garden window. Despite everything, she'd had a nice day. Had her engagement to Murat been real, she would have been delighted to know that these women would be a part of her life.

But it wasn't real, and their theory that Murat's pride had kept him from holding on to her was nice to think about but was not in any way true.

"Not that it matters now," she whispered. Somehow she'd managed to get over him. At least she didn't have to worry about that now. Her feelings weren't engaged and her heart was firmly out of reach. She was going to make sure things stayed that way.

Daphne planned a quiet remainder of the day. She assumed Murat wouldn't come back to torment her until the morning, and she was partially right. Around four the gold doors opened again, but instead of the crown prince, she saw the king.

"Your Majesty," she said, coming to her feet before dropping into a low curtsy.

"Daphne."

Murat's father walked toward her and held out both his hands. He captured hers and kissed her knuckles. "How lovely to have you back in Bahania." The handsome older man chuckled. "Most young women today don't know the first thing about a good curtsy, but you've always had style."

"I had several years of training in etiquette. Some of it had to rub off," she said with a smile. While she might not be excited about what Murat was up to, she couldn't help being pleased at seeing the king. He had always been very kind to her, especially when she'd been young, in love and terrified.

"Come," King Hassan said as he led her to the cluster of sofas. "Tell me everything. You and your family are well?"

"Everyone is great." Except for Laurel who was furious about Brittany not marrying Murat. "They send their best." Or they would have if they'd known she would be speaking with the king.

"I'm sure they're very excited about what has happened."

Her good mood slipped. "Yes. My parents are delighted."

King Hassan had to be close to sixty, but he looked much younger. There was an air of strength about him. Authority and determination. No doubt that came from a royal lineage that stretched back over a thousand years. He was considered one of the most forward-thinking leaders in the world. A king who earned his people's respect through his actions and loyalty to his country.

Murat would be equally as excellent a leader, Daphne thought. He'd been born to the position and had never once stumbled. Which made him admirable, but not someone she wanted to marry.

"My son sends you a surprise," the king said as the gold doors opened again.

Servants appeared with the carts they seemed to

favor. But this time instead of food they brought clay and sculpting tools.

Her fingers instantly itched for the feel of clay, while the cynical part of her brain wondered if he thought he could bribe her with her hobby.

"You must thank him for me," she said as the servants bowed and left.

"You can thank him yourself. He'll be by later."

Oh, joy, she thought as she smiled politely.

"You are aware of the date," King Hassan said.

Daphne blinked at him. "Today's date?"

"No. That the wedding date has been set. It is in four months. The challenge will be to get everything done in such a short period of time, but I am sure that with the right staff, we will be successful."

She stiffened her spine and drew in a breath. "Your Majesty, I mean no disrespect, but the problem isn't finding the right staff. The problem is I am not going to marry Murat, and there is nothing anyone can say to convince me otherwise."

She'd thought the monarch might be surprised, but he only chuckled. "Ah, two stubborn people. So who will win this battle?"

"I will. It is the old story of the rabbit and the hound. The rabbit gets away because while the hound runs for its supper, the rabbit runs for its life."

"An interesting point." The king took her hand again and lightly squeezed her fingers. "I have often wondered how things would have been different if you had stayed and married Murat. Have you?"

"No." Well, maybe a little, but she wasn't interested in admitting it. "I wasn't ready to be married. I was too young, as was your son. The position of his wife requires much, and I'm not sure I would have been up to the task."

"Perhaps. There are many responsibilities in being queen, although your questions and self-doubts make me think you would have done well in the position. He never married."

Daphne drew her hand from his and laced her fingers together on her lap. "Murat? I'm aware of that. Had he married I would not currently be a prisoner in the harem."

"You know that is not my point," Hassan said humorously. "You never married, either."

"I've been busy with my studies and establishing my career."

"It is not much of an excuse. Perhaps each of you were waiting for the other to make the first move."

Daphne nearly sprang to her feet. At the last second she remembered that action would be a fairly serious breach of protocol. "I assure you that is not even close to true. Murat has enjoyed the company of so many beautiful women, I doubt he remembers them all, let alone a young woman from a decade ago."

"And now?" the king asked.

"We barely know each other."

"An excellent point. Perhaps this is a good time to change that." The king rose. "Murat wants this wedding, Daphne, as do your parents. As do I. Are you willing to take on the world?"

She stood and tried not to give in to the sudden rush of fear. "If I have to."

"Perhaps it would be easier to give in graciously. Would marriage to Murat be so horrible?"

"Yes. I think it would be." She bit her lower lip. "Your Majesty, would you really force me to marry your son against my will?"

His dark eyes never wavered as he spoke. "If I have to."

Murat found Daphne in the garden. The sun had nearly slipped below the horizon, and the first whispers of the cool evening air whispered against his face.

She sat on a stone bench, her shoulders slumped, her chin nearly touching her chest. The only word that came to his mind at that moment was...*broken*.

He hurried forward and pulled her to her feet. She gasped in surprise, but didn't resist until he tried to draw her close.

"What do you think you're doing?" she demanded, twisting free of his embrace.

"Comforting you."

She glared at him. "You're the source of my troubles, not the relief from them."

"I'm all you have."

She took a step back. "What a sorry state of affairs. What on earth does that sentence say about my life?"

"That at least there is one person on your side."

Little light spilled into the garden, but there was enough for him to see her beautiful features. Her wide eyes had darkened with pain and confusion. Her full lips trembled. It was as if the weight of the world pressed down upon her, and he ached for her.

"Come," he said, holding out his arms. "You'll feel better."

"Maybe I don't want to," she said stubbornly, even as she moved forward and leaned against him.

He wrapped his arms around her. She was slight, so delicate and yet so strong. She smelled of flowers and soap and of herself. That arousing fragrance he had never been able to forget.

Wanting filled him, but something else, as well. Something that made this moment feel right.

He felt her hands on his back, and she rested her forehead against his shoulder.

"No one will help me," she said. "I've been making phone calls for nearly two hours. Not my family— which isn't a big surprise—nor any of my friends. I even called my congressman. Everyone thinks us getting married is a fine idea. They refused to believe that I'm being held against my will, and they all hinted for an invitation to the wedding."

"Then you may add them to the list."

She raised her head. Tears glittered in her eyes. "That's not what I wanted to hear."

He knew what she wanted him to say, but he would not speak the words. To set her free…it would not happen.

"You will enjoy being queen," he said. "There is much power in the position."

"I've never been that interested in power."

"You've never had it before."

"Murat, you know this is wrong."

"Why? You are to marry me, Crown Prince Murat. It is not as if you're being asked to wed a used-camel dealer."

She gave a half laugh, half sob and pushed away from him. The tears had trickled down her face. He wiped them away with his fingers.

"Do not cry," he murmured. "I offer you the world."

"I only want my freedom."

"To do what? To give shots to overweight dogs and cats? Here you can make a difference. Here you will be a part of history. Your children and grandchildren will rule this land."

"It's not enough."

He growled low in his throat. Had she always been this stubborn? Was she trying to punish him for what had happened before? All right. Perhaps he could give a little on that point.

"Why did you leave me?" he asked. "Before. Ten years ago. Why did you go?"

Her shoulders slumped again, and the pain returned to her eyes. "It doesn't matter."

"Yes, it does. I wish to know."

"You wouldn't understand."

"Then explain it to me. I am very intelligent."

"Not about me." She swallowed. "Murat, you have to let me go."

Instead of answering her statement, he stepped forward and kissed her. He caught her by surprise—he could tell by the sudden intake of air and the way she hesitated before responding. But instead of retreating, he settled his hand on her hip and the back of her neck and brushed his tongue against her lower lip.

She parted instantly. As he swept inside he felt the heat flaring between them. Wanting poured through him, making it difficult to hold back when he wanted to rip off her clothing and claim her right there on the bench.

Instead he continued to kiss her, moving slowly, retreating, pulling back until she was the one to grab him and deepen the embrace. When he finally straightened, she looked as aroused as he felt.

"You see," he said, "there is much between us. We will take the time to get to know each other better. That will make you comfortable with the thought of our marriage."

"Don't bet on it," she said, but her swollen mouth and passion-filled eyes betrayed her.

Murat brushed her cheek with his fingers, then walked out of the harem. Victory was at hand. He would wear away Daphne's defenses until she understood that their marriage was inevitable. Then she would acquiesce and they would be wed. She would love him and be happy and he...

He stepped through the gold doors and into the hallway. He would return to his regular life, content, but untouched by the experience.

Chapter Six

Daphne rolled the cool clay in her hands until the combination of heat from her skin and the friction of the action caused the thick rope to yield to her will. She tore off a piece of clay and pressed it flat, then added it to the sculpture in progress.

The half-finished project had finally begun to take shape. There was a sense of movement in the way the man leaned too far to the right. His body was still a squarish lump, but she knew how she would slice away the excess clay and mold what was left. The head would follow, with the arms and the tray of dishes to come last. The tray that would be on the verge of tumbling to the ground.

Around her, the garden vibrated with life. She heard the chatter of the parrots and the rustle of small creatures hiding in the thick foliage. Several of the king's cats stretched out in the sun, the slow rise and fall of their chests the only sign of life.

As far as prisons went, this wasn't a bad one, Daphne told herself, as she picked up another clump of clay. Not that she had a whole lot of experience with which to compare. She'd never been held against her will before. Still, if one had to be, the Bahania harem was the place.

She couldn't complain about the service, either. Delicious meals appeared whenever she requested them. Her large bed was plenty comfortable, and the bathroom was so luxurious that it bordered on sinful. Still, none of these pleasures made up for the fact that she had been confined against her will with the threat of marriage to Murat hanging over her head.

He had spoken of getting to know each other, but she wasn't so sure that was a good idea. Men like him didn't make a habit of letting just anyone see the inner person, and she doubted their engagement gave her extra privileges in that area. Which left her with the distinct impression that his request had been a lot more about giving himself time to convince her that this was a good idea than any desire he had to share his feelings.

Even more annoying was the fact that a part of her *was* interested in learning more about the man. Life was never easy when the one who got away was a future king.

She picked up a sharp piece of wood that was part

knife, part chisel and went to work on the torso of the sculpture. When the rough shape was correct, she added features to the head, creating a face that was a fair representation of the man in question. A smile pulled at her mouth. She only had to complete the arms and the tray.

"Men have died for less."

Daphne heard the voice about the same time the sound of footsteps entered her consciousness. She'd been so focused on her work that she hadn't been paying attention. Now she pressed clay into the shape of a tray and did her best not to react to Murat's nearness.

"I thought there was artistic freedom here in Bahania," she said, not looking up from her clay.

"Most artists are too intelligent to mock me."

Daphne spared him a glance. As always he wore a suit, although this time he'd left the jacket behind. The crisp white shirt he wore contrasted with his dark skin. He'd rolled the sleeves up to the elbow, and she found the sight of his bare forearms oddly erotic.

Sheesh. She really had to get out more.

"My intelligence has never been an issue," she said. "Do you doubt it now?"

He glanced at the tray taking shape in her hands. "You sculpt me carrying dishes?"

She grinned. "Actually I sculpt you about to drop the dishes you're carrying. There's a difference."

He made a noise low in his throat, which she knew she should take for displeasure, but there was something about it that made her stomach clench. Perhaps the noise was too close to desire.

Stop that! She grabbed hold of any wayward emotions and reminded herself she needed to keep things firmly in check. Wanting Murat wasn't in the rules. It would only make things difficult and awkward. Hadn't she already had to deal with a broken heart once where he was concerned? Was she really willing to forget that the man held her prisoner and threatened a wedding, regardless of her wishes?

"Why are you here?" she asked as she felt her temper grow and with it her strength to resist him.

"Am I not allowed to come and visit with my bride?"

She rolled her eyes and set down the small tray. Next up she began to form tiny glasses and plates.

"I will take your silence as agreement," he said.

"You may take it any way you'd like, but you'd be wrong."

He sighed. "You are most difficult."

"Tell me about it. Of course you've made 'difficult' an art form. I'm still little more than a student."

He ignored that, saying nothing as he walked around her and the sculpture. "You have an energy I haven't seen before," he said. "Perhaps you needed this time to relax."

Perhaps, but she wasn't about to admit that to him. "Is there a point to your visit or are you simply here to annoy me?"

"You will be visited by someone later."

"The first of three ghosts?"

He frowned slightly, then his expression cleared. "Are you in need of a visit by the ghosts of Christmas past, present and future?"

"No. I've always kept the spirit of Christmas in my heart."

"I am pleased to hear it is so. That will bode well for our children. They will have a festive season to look forward to."

Her jaw clenched. "Is this where I point out, yet again, that I haven't agreed to marry you, nor am I likely to?"

"You may if it makes you happy. However, I will not listen. Instead I will inform you that Mr. Peterson is an old and valued member of our staff here. He specializes in coordinating formal state events."

She got it right away. "Like weddings."

"Exactly. I would appreciate it if you were polite and cooperative."

She formed a tiny clay bowl and set it on the tray. "I would appreciate being set free. It seems we are both destined for disappointment."

Murat moved closer. "Why do you attempt to thwart me?"

"Because I can't seem to get through to you any other way." She wiped her hands on the damp towel on her workbench, then turned to face him. "I don't get it, Murat. What's in this for you?" She held up her hand. "Spare me the party line about marriage and destiny or whatever. Why on earth are you insisting on marrying a woman who doesn't want you?"

Her gaze met Murat's with a familiarity that should have annoyed him, but this was Daphne, and he found himself enjoying most everything she did. Even her challenges.

He smiled as he moved close, crowding her. Daphne, being stubborn and difficult *and* predictable, didn't move back. She made it so easy, he thought with pleasure. He liked that about her.

"You claim not to want me," he murmured as he cupped her head in one hand and bent low to kiss her. "Your body tells me otherwise."

Then, before she could speak whatever nonsense she had in mind, he brushed his mouth against hers.

She squirmed, but he wove his fingers through her hair to hold her in place. When she pressed her lips together to resist his claim on her, he chuckled, then raised his free hand to her breast.

Instantly she gasped. He took advantage of her parted lips and swept inside. At the same time, he brushed his thumb against her hard nipple.

She held out against him for the space of a heartbeat before she wrapped her arms around his neck and surrendered. Her mouth softened against him, her tongue greeted him with an erotic dance, and her entire body melted into his.

Heat exploded between them, and Murat found himself fighting his own desire. He had touched her in an effort to teach her a lesson, but now he was the one being schooled on the power of unfulfilled need.

Her hands clutched at him, pulling him closer. She tilted her head and deepened the kiss, even as she pressed into his hand. He explored her breast and found himself hungering to know the taste of her hot skin.

But that was not for now, he reminded himself as he

gathered the strength to step back. He would know her soon enough—once she understood that their marriage was as inevitable as the tide.

"You see," he said with a calmness he did not feel. "You *do* want me."

She shook her head as if to clear her thoughts. Her eyes were large and unfocused, her face flushed.

"There's a difference between wanting a man in my bed for a couple of weeks and wanting him in my life permanently," she said, her voice low and angry. "If you were trying to prove a point, I'm not impressed."

"Your body says otherwise."

"Fortunately I make my decisions with my brain."

"Your brain wants me, as well," he told her. "You resist only to be stubborn. I am pleased the sexual spark has lasted so long between us. It bodes well for our marriage. You will be a good wife and provide me with many strong, healthy, intelligent children, including an heir to carry on the monarchy."

"And my reward in all this is your pleasure. Gee, how thrilling."

He refused to be provoked by her. "Your reward is in the honor I bestow upon you. I believe you already understand that, and in time you will grow more comfortable showing me your pleasure in your situation."

She opened her mouth, then closed it. He could almost see the steam building up inside of her.

"Of all the arrogant, egotistical, annoying things you've ever said to me," she began.

He cut her off with a wave of his hand. "Say what

you like, but I know the truth. You're already begging to love me. In a matter of weeks you will want nothing but the pleasure of being near me."

"When pigs fly."

Daphne thought Murat was assuming an awful lot, especially that she was interested in him sexually. Whatever warm and yummy feelings he'd generated a couple of minutes ago with his hot kisses and knowing hands, he'd destroyed with a few badly chosen words.

"I wouldn't marry you if you were the last man alive. I said no before, I'm saying no again. No. No!"

The infuriating man simply smiled. "Mr. Peterson will be here shortly. I trust you will act appropriately."

Anger filled her. She reached for something to throw, but there was only her clay statue, and she loved it too much to smash it.

"Get out!" she yelled.

"As you wish, my bride."

She screamed and grabbed the remaining block of clay. When she turned back, Murat had already walked toward the harem itself. Even though she knew she couldn't throw that far, she pitched the clay at him and had the satisfaction of hearing it splat on the stone path.

"I'll get you for this," she vowed. Somehow, some way, she would come up with a plan, and he would be sorry he'd ever tried to mess with her.

Mr. Peterson might be old and valued but he was also the prissiest man Daphne had ever met.

He was small—maybe five-four—so she towered

over him even in low-heeled sandals. He had the deli-
cate bone structure of a bird, with tiny hands and feet.
Next to him she felt like an awkward and ill-mannered
Amazon giant.

"Ms. Snowden," he said as he entered the harem and
bowed. "It is more than a great pleasure to meet you."

She wasn't sure how it could be *more* than a great
pleasure, but she wasn't the fancy-party expert.

"The pleasure is mine," she said as she led the way
to the sitting area and motioned to the collection of
sofas there.

Mr. Peterson looked them over closely, then chose
the one that was lowest to the floor. No doubt he hated
when his feet dangled.

She sat across from him and wondered how badly
this was going to go. Mr. Peterson wanted to plan a wedding and she didn't. That was bound to create some
friction.

"We're working on a very tight schedule," he began
as he set his briefcase on the table in front of him and
opened the locks with a click.

She noticed that the silk hankie in his jacket breast
pocket perfectly matched his tie. He sounded as if he'd
been born in Britain but hadn't lived there in a number
of years. Perhaps he'd moved here with his parents back
in the eighteenth century.

"Prince Murat informed me that the wedding will be
in four months," he said. "I'll be providing you with historical information on previous weddings, along with my
list of suggestions on flower choices and the like. Some

of my ideas may seem silly to a modern young woman such as yourself, but we have a history here in Bahania. A long and honorable history that needs to be respected."

He drew in his breath for what she assumed would be another long speech specifically designed to make her feel like a twelve-year-old who had just spilled fruit punch on a very important houseguest.

She decided it was time to change the direction of the conversation.

"There isn't going to be a wedding," she said, and had the satisfaction of watching Mr. Peterson freeze in place.

It was amazing. The man didn't breathe or move or do anything but sit there, one hand grasping a sheath of papers, another reaching for a pen. At last he blinked.

"Excuse me?"

"No wedding," she said, speaking slowly. "I'm not marrying Murat."

"Prince Murat," he said.

He was correcting her address of the man who wanted to marry her?

"Prince or not, there's no engagement."

"I see."

She doubted that. "So there's no point in us having this conversation. I do appreciate that you were willing to stop by though. It was very kind of you."

She offered a bright smile in the hopes that the little man would simply stand and leave. But of course her luck wasn't that good.

"Prince Murat assures me that—"

"I know what he told you and what he's thinking, but

he's wrong. No wedding. *N-O* on the wedding front. Am I making myself clear?"

Mr. Peterson obviously hadn't been expecting a reluctant bride. He fussed with his papers for a few seconds, then picked up his pen. "About the guest list. I was told you come from a large and distinguished family. Do you have any idea how many of them will be attending?"

Daphne sighed. So Mr. Peterson had decided to simply ignore her claims and move forward.

"Ms. Snowden?" he prodded. "How many family members."

"Not a clue," she told him cheerfully.

"Will you be providing me with a guest list of any kind?"

"Nope."

The little man shook his head. "If necessary I can contact your mother."

"I'm sure you can." And her mother would be delighted by the question and the chance to influence the wedding.

Wasn't it enough that Murat insisted on this charade? How far was he willing to take it?

"Excuse me," she said as she rose to her feet. "I need to put a stop to this right now."

She walked toward the door and once she got there, she simply pushed it open.

The cross bar wasn't in place, no doubt so Mr. Peterson could leave when he was finished. There were only two guards on duty and neither of them looked as if they'd expected her to come strolling out of the harem.

When they saw her, they glanced at each other, as if uncertain about what to do.

Daphne took advantage of their confusion and started running. She made it halfway down the long hall before she heard footsteps racing after her. Up ahead the elevator beckoned like a beacon of freedom.

"Be there, be there," she chanted as she ran. She skidded to a stop in front of the doors and pushed the Up button. Thankfully, the doors immediately slid open.

She stepped inside and pressed the button for the second floor and watched as the doors closed in the faces of the guards.

Ha! She'd escaped. Probably not for long, but the feel of freedom was heady.

She exited on the second floor and hurried toward the business wing of the palace. She had a vague recollection of the way from her detailed explorations ten years ago. At a T-intersection, she hesitated, not sure which way to go, then followed a young man in a tailored suit as he turned left.

Seconds later she entered a large, round foyer. A middle-aged man sat at the desk and raised his eyebrows inquiringly.

"Crown Prince Murat," she said.

"Is he expecting you?"

In the distance she heard running feet. The guards, no doubt. She suspected reinforcements had been called.

"I'm his fiancée," she said briskly.

The man straightened in his seat. "Yes. Of course,

Ms. Snowden. Down that hallway, to your left. There are guards at the door. You can't miss it. If you'll give me a moment, I'll escort you there myself."

"No need," she said, taking off in the direction he'd indicated. She saw massive, carved, dark wood double doors and two guards standing on duty. One of them had his fingers pressed to his ear as if he were listening to something. When he saw her, he spoke quickly.

"I'm going in there," she said as she hurried toward the doors. "And you can't stop me."

The guards stepped forward and actually drew their weapons. A cold blade of fear sliced through her midsection.

"Murat isn't going to be very happy if you shoot me," she said, hoping it was true.

The guards moved toward her.

More footsteps thundered from behind, and she was seconds from being trapped.

"Murat!" she screamed as one of the men reached for her.

The huge door on the right opened and Murat stalked out.

"What is going on here?" he demanded. He glanced at the guards, then settled his stern gaze on her. "Release her at once."

The man did so, and Daphne quickly stepped behind Murat. "I escaped," she murmured in his ear. "That made them cranky."

He looked at her and raised one eyebrow. "I see. And Mr. Peterson?"

"We didn't much get along. All he wanted to talk about was the wedding, and I kept saying there wasn't going to be one. It wasn't very pleasant for either of us."

Murat didn't respond verbally. Instead he took her by the hand and led her into his office.

"Stay here," he said as he placed her in the center of an exceptionally beautiful rug. "I will return shortly."

With that he turned and left. She heard him speaking with the guards.

Daphne glanced around at the large office, noting the beautifully carved desk and the view of the gardens. None of the royal family had offices that faced away from the palace grounds. Years ago Murat had told her it was for security reasons. She'd been afraid for him at the time, but he had smiled and pulled her close and told her not to worry.

She shook off the memory. Murat returned and closed the door behind him.

"You are safe for now," he said. "I'll be having an interesting talk with my security team later. They should not have let you escape."

"Points for me," she said.

"Interesting that in your moment of freedom, you chose to run here. To me."

"Don't read too much into it. I didn't come here for a good reason."

"No? Then why?"

"Because I want to talk about the wedding, or lack thereof. You can't make me do it, Murat."

He moved close and touched her cheek. She hated how her body instantly went up in flames.

"You enjoy challenging me," he said. "However, I think the real problem lies elsewhere. You have been cooped up for too long. Go change your clothes, and we'll take a ride into the desert."

"And if I don't want to go?" she asked.

He looked at her. "Do you?"

She remembered those long-ago desert rides. The scent of the fresh air, the movement of the horse, and the beauty all around her.

"I do, but I hate that you assume you know best."

"I *do* know best. Now return to the harem and change your clothes. I'll meet you downstairs in thirty minutes."

"Does this mean I'm allowed to roam freely about the palace?"

He grinned. "Not even on a bet."

Chapter Seven

Daphne settled into the saddle and breathed in the fresh air. She'd been spending plenty of time outdoors in the harem garden but for some reason, everything seemed better, brighter now that she was sitting on a horse about to ride into the desert on a great adventure. Or to the nearest oasis, whichever came first.

There were a thousand reasons to still be angry with Murat—not the least was the man continued to hold her prisoner and insist they were to be married. Somehow none of that mattered anymore. At least not right now. She wanted to ride fast and feel the wind in her hair. She wanted to spin in circles on the sand, her arms outstretched, until she was too dizzy to stand. She wanted to drink cool, clear water from an underground spring and taste life. Then she would be mad at him again.

"Ready?" he asked.

She nodded as she pulled her hat lower over her forehead. All the sunscreen in the world couldn't completely protect her fair skin. So to keep herself from reaching the crone years too early, she'd worn a loose fitting, long-sleeved white shirt and a hat. Beside her, Murat looked handsome and timeless in his black riding pants and tailored white shirt. His black stallion was so large and difficult to manage as to be a cliché. Her own mount, a gray gelding of particularly fine build, also danced impatiently but with a little more restraint.

"When did you last ride?" Murat asked, as he urged his horse forward. The stallion leaped ahead several feet before agreeing to a more sedate walk.

"A couple of months ago. I usually go regularly, but I've been caught up with work."

"Then we will take things easily. This is unfamiliar country."

She glanced at him from under her lashes. "I don't mind if we go fast."

He grinned. "Of course you don't. But we will wait until you find your seat again."

She wanted to point out that she hadn't lost it in the first place—it was where it had always been. But she knew what he meant. That she had to get comfortable on her horse. So she contented herself with enjoying the scenery.

The royal stable sat on the edge of the desert, about

a forty-minute drive from the Pink Palace. Daphne knew she could happily spend her life there, studying bloodlines and planning future generations of amazing Arabian horses. Not that she wanted Murat to know. He had too much power already—he didn't need to discover more of her weaknesses.

She glanced around as the last bits of civilization gave way to the wildness of the desert. When their horses stepped onto sand, she couldn't help laughing out loud.

"Whatever you thought about me," Murat said. "You always loved Bahania."

"I agree."

"You should have returned for a visit."

"Somehow that didn't seem exactly wise."

"Did you think I would make things difficult?"

She wasn't sure how to answer that. If she said yes, it implied that he had cared for her after she left and she didn't think that was true. If she said no, she risked going in the opposite direction and she didn't think Murat would like that. As a rule, she didn't much care about what he liked, but this afternoon was different. For once, she didn't want to fight.

"I thought it might make things awkward," she admitted.

"That is a possibility," he said, surprising her. "But it is sad that you could not see this for so long."

She glanced around at the beauty of the desert and had to agree. She loved the rolling hills that gave way to vast stretches of emptiness. She loved the tiny creatures who managed to thrive in such harsh surroundings.

Most of all she loved coming upon an oasis—a gift from God plopped down in the middle of nothing.

"You can taste the history out here," she said, thinking of all the generations who had walked this exact path and seen these same sights.

"We are closer to the past in the desert. I can feel my heritage all around me."

She grinned. "You come from a long line of men compelled to steal or kidnap their brides. Why is that? Are you all genetically unable to woo women in a normal way?"

He made a noise low in his throat. Daphne grinned.

"I'm serious," she said.

"No, you are tweaking the tiger's tail. Take care that he doesn't turn on you and gobble you up."

As Murat wasn't an actual tiger, she didn't have to worry about being eaten. Instead his words painted a picture of a different kind of devouring…one that involved bodies and touching and exquisite feelings of passion and surrender.

A dull ache settled in her stomach, making her shift on the saddle. Probably best not to think about that sort of thing, she told herself. Under the circumstances, sleeping with Murat would be a disaster. He would take her sexual surrender as a resounding "yes" on the marriage front.

But she couldn't help wondering what he would be like in bed. So far his kisses had reduced her to a quivering mass. Ten years ago she'd been too innocent and out of her element to be much more than intimidated by the obvious sexual experience of the man. Now she found herself wanting to sign up for a weekend seminar on the subject.

Next time, she promised herself. When her future and her freedom weren't on the line.

"Those marriages you mentioned may have started in violence, but they all ended happily."

She glanced at him. "You know this how?"

"There are letters and diaries."

"I'd like to read them sometime," she said. "Not that I don't trust you to tell me the truth…" She smiled. "Well, I don't, actually."

"You think I would lie?"

"I think you would stretch the truth if it suited your purpose."

He muttered something she couldn't hear. "How do you explain a relationship that lasts thirty or forty years and produces so many children?"

"Women don't have to be happy to get pregnant."

"I will give you the diaries," he said. "You will see for yourself that you misjudge my ancestors as much as you misjudge me. Are you ready to go faster?"

The quick change in subject caught her unaware, but she immediately nodded her agreement.

"I'm fine," she said. "Lead the way."

He nodded then urged his horse forward. The powerful stallion leaped from walking to a gallop. Her horse followed.

Daphne leaned forward into the powerful gait. The ground seemed to blur as they raced across the open area. She wanted to laugh from the pleasure of the moment.

Pure freedom, she thought, wishing there was more of this in her regular life. But her rides were sedate, on trails in well-known areas. There was little left to discover outside of Chicago.

Unlike here, where the desert kept secrets for thousands of years. While she could trace her family history back to the early 1700s, Murat could trace his for a millennium.

His name would be carved in the walls of the palace. His likeness stored, his life remembered. He had offered all that to her, as well. The privilege of being a part of Bahanian history. Her body could have been the safe haven of future kings yet to be born.

They sped across the desert for several miles. At last Murat slowed his mount and hers followed suit.

"We will walk them now," he said. "Allow them to cool down. We are close to the oasis."

She nodded, still caught up in her thoughts. What would it be like to be a part of something this amazing? Ten years ago she'd never considered all that he offered. Lately it seemed she could think of nothing else.

"The light is gone from your eyes," he said. "What troubles you?"

"I'm not troubled, just thoughtful."

"Tell me what you have on your mind."

She looked at him, at his handsome, chiseled face, at the power in his body and the authority he wore like a second skin.

"You are Crown Prince Murat of Bahania," she said.

"You will one day rule all that we see and miles beyond. You come from a history that stretches back through the ages to a time when my ancestors lived in huts and shivered through the winter. Why on earth would you choose me to share all this? Why me? Why not someone else?"

Murat didn't look at her. Instead he stared straight ahead. There was no way to tell what he was thinking.

"The oasis is just up there," he said, pointing to the right. "Over that dune."

"You're not going to answer my question?"

"No."

She wanted to push him for the truth, but at the same time, felt a reluctance to do so. There were many things she didn't want to discuss, including the fact—which he'd already pointed out—that when she'd burst free of the harem, instead of heading out of the palace, she'd run directly to the man holding her prisoner. Talk about a mixed message.

They rode in silence until they reached the oasis. Daphne stared at the small refuge in the desert, taking in the cluster of palm and date trees, the clear blue water gently lapping against the grass-covered shore and the bushes that seemed to provide a screen of privacy.

"Lovely," she said as she dismounted and pulled off her hat.

"I am glad you are pleased."

"Oh, yeah, because my pleasure makes your day."

She meant the comment as flip and teasing, but Murat didn't smile.

"Perhaps it does," he said. "Perhaps that is what you don't understand."

Before she could absorb what he'd just said, let alone think up a response, he led his horse over to a patch of shade. "We will rest here before heading back."

She followed. When he stopped, she turned to her horse and began stroking the animal's neck.

"Good, strong boy," she murmured as she examined the shoulder muscles, then bent down to run her hands along the well-formed front legs.

"I assure you I have a most capable staff in my stable," Murat said.

She straightened. "Oh. Sorry. Occupational hazard. I can't help checking." She patted the horse's side. "He's in great shape. Just like the cats back at the palace."

"I will be sure to pass along your compliments," Murat said dryly.

She loosely tied the horse to a tree, then joined Murat as he walked toward the water.

"It's quiet," she said.

"Yes. That is why I enjoy coming here."

She glanced around. "No guards?"

"This area is patrolled regularly, but at the moment we are alone." He glanced at her. "If you wish to kill me, now is the time."

"Good to know, but I'm not that annoyed. Yet."

He smiled. "How you continue to challenge me, but we both know who will be victorious in the end."

"Not you."

"Exactly me." He moved close and stared down at her. "Your surrender is at hand. Do you not feel it?"

What she felt was a trickle of something that could very well have been anticipation slipping down her spine. Her skin got all hot and prickly and she had the incredibly irrational urge to throw herself into his arms and beg for a surrender of another kind. Or maybe that was the surrender he meant. In which case she was more than willing to be the one giving in.

"I'm not going to marry you," she said.

He rested his hands on her shoulders. "You say the same thing over and over. It grows most tiresome."

"That's because you're not listening. If you were, I'd stop having to say it."

"How like a woman to make it the man's fault."

"How like a man to be stubborn and unreasonable."

"I am very reasonable. Right now you want me, and I intend to let you have me."

Before she could even gasp in outrage, he claimed her mouth with his. His firm, warm lips caressed her own until she felt compelled to wrap her arms around his neck and never let go. The outrage melted away.

He kissed her gently, teasing her with light brushes that made her nerve endings tingle. He stroked her lower lip with his tongue, but when she parted for him he nipped her instead of entering. He dropped his hands to her hips and drew her against him so that her belly pressed flat against his arousal.

The hardness there made her gasp, but again he chose not to take advantage of her invitation. Instead he kissed along her jaw and nibbled the sensitive skin under her ear. He made her squirm and gasp as need swept through her with the driving force of a sandstorm. He licked her earlobe, then traced a path down the side of her neck to the V of her shirt where he sucked gently on her skin.

She felt hot and uncomfortable, as if she'd been wound too tight. Her breasts ached, her thighs trembled, and she really wanted the man to kiss her.

Unable to control herself any longer, she dropped her hands to his face and drew his head up.

"Now," she said, her voice low and impatient.

"As you wish," he murmured right before he claimed her mouth.

This time he did as she wanted. He swept inside with the purposeful intent of a man set on pleasing a woman. He circled her tongue with his own. He explored and danced and surged until she was breathless with wanting.

His hands moved from her hips to her back. One slipped around to her waist and she caught her breath in anticipation as he moved higher and higher. Closer until he at last cupped her breast in his long, lean fingers.

The pressure was unbearably perfect, she thought through a haze of desire. As his fingers brushed against her tight nipples, she withdrew from the kiss so she could focus completely on his touch. Her breathing increased. She looped her arms around his neck and held on as her knees began to give way.

He brought up his other hand so he could cup both breasts. The delicious torture make her shiver. He raised his head and looked into her eyes.

"You are more beautiful than the dawn," he whispered. "I feel you respond to me. Can you deny what you want?"

She shook her head.

At that moment she had the sense she could disappear into his dark eyes and that it wouldn't be such a bad fate. Not if there were nights filled with this kind of attention. Not if he kept touching her.

She felt her body swelling in anticipation. Her panties dampened as flesh begged and wept for release.

He moved to the buttons on her shirt and quickly unfastened them. But he only went down to the waistband of her jeans and didn't bother pulling the shirt free. Which meant when he tugged the garment down her shoulders, he pinned her arms at her side.

She knew she could free herself with a quick jerk against the fabric, but for the moment, she felt oddly trapped. As if she were at his mercy. As if he could take her against her will.

Crazy, she told herself. Yet…oddly erotic.

He moved to the hook between her breasts and unfastened it. She watched as he slipped the bra away, exposing her skin to sun and air…and to his heated gaze.

He stared at her like a hungry man facing a last meal. Slowly he traced her curves, touching so lightly he almost tickled her. When he touched the tip of his finger against the very tip of her nipple, she felt the jolt clear down to her thighs.

She groaned. His breathing increased, then he bent low and drew her nipple into his mouth.

The combination of damp heat and gentle sucking nearly sent her to her knees. She struggled to free herself from her shirt so she could cling to him. The wanting grew. She didn't remember ever being this aroused before. She wasn't sure it was possible to need so much and stay conscious.

At last she was able to pull her shirt free of her jeans. She shrugged out of it and her bra, then clutched his head, holding him in place against her breasts.

"More," she breathed as he circled with his tongue.

Tension filled her body. She felt herself getting closer and closer to her release. Passion spiraled out of control.

With her free hand, she tugged at his shirt. He straightened and pulled it off in one easy, graceful movement. Then he stood before her, bare-chested, his arousal clearly outlined in his dark slacks.

"Tell me you want me," he demanded.

"How can you doubt it?"

"Say the words."

She stared into his dark eyes and knew that there was no going back. She had to know what it felt like to make love with Murat. She had to have that memory to take with her when she left.

"I want you."

For a heartbeat he did nothing. Then he gathered her up in his arms and lowered her to the ground.

"We must be practical," he said as he sat next to her. "Riding boots are not romantic."

She grinned as he pulled his off, then went to work

on her. When their feet were bare, she stretched out on his shirt and held open her arms.

"Make love with me, Murat."

He claimed her with a soul-touching kiss and a growl. His clever fingers returned to her breasts where he teased her into a frenzy. She squirmed and writhed, wanting more, needing more to find her release.

At last he moved lower, to the button of her jeans. He unfastened it and lowered the zipper. She pushed down with him, helping him remove the heavy fabric, along with her panties.

And then she was naked before him. Rather than feel embarrassed, Daphne let her legs fall open in a brazen invitation for what she really wanted. He did not disappoint. Even as he lowered his head and began to kiss her breasts, he slipped his fingers between her thighs and into her waiting dampness.

He found that one perfect spot on the first try. Just the slight brush of skin against the swollen knot of nerves made her jump. He shifted slightly so that he could rub that spot with his thumb while slipping his fingers deep inside her.

This was too much, she thought as she found herself caught up in a sensual vortex. His mouth on her breasts, his thumb rubbing, his fingers moving around and around. She was slick and more than ready, and it was just a matter of seconds until the tension filled her.

She tried to hold back, to breathe, to do anything to keep herself from falling so quickly. But it felt too good. She clutched at him and gave up the battle.

"Now!" she gasped as her release washed over her. Wave after wave of pleasure surrounded her, filled her, caught her and then let her fall. She pulsed her hips in time with his movements, slowing as she neared the end. He slowed, as well.

When she'd finished, she sank back onto his shirt and draped one forearm across her eyes. It was one thing to impulsively give in to sex with a man. It was another when he was as imperious as Murat. What would happen now?

She braced herself for some comment about his prowess with women or how easily she'd surrendered, and tried to tell herself it didn't matter.

But he said nothing.

The silence grew until Daphne finally dropped her arm and opened her eyes. Murat leaned over her, but he didn't look overly pleased with himself. Instead he seemed…humbled.

No way, she thought, even as he brushed his mouth against hers.

"Thank you," he said quietly.

She blinked. "Excuse me?"

"Thank you for letting me pleasure you. I know that you could have held back and kept me from taking you to paradise, and you did not."

The man was crazy. She could no more have held back than she could have flown to the moon. But he didn't have to know that.

"I liked what you were doing," she said.

"Perhaps you would like something else, as well."

She thought about how hard he'd been, how long and thick. Then she thought about him inside of her.

"I think I would," she told him with a smile.

He didn't have to be asked twice. Seconds later he was naked and kneeling between her knees. He braced himself on his hands and slowly entered her.

He felt exactly right, she thought as she reached up to caress his back. When he filled her, nerve endings cheered and began to do a little dance. Despite her first release, she felt the tension building again and knew it was going to be even better the second time around.

He moved slowly, giving them both time to adjust and anticipate. About the third time he stroked all the way in, she gave up acting like a lady and pulled him down against her. He wrapped his arms around her and kissed her. As their tongues mated, she shifted so she could hug his hips with her legs. That caused him to push in even deeper and she was instantly lost.

Murat felt the first pulsing ripples of Daphne's release. His plans to dazzle her with his stamina quickly faded as each contraction pushed him closer to the edge. She gasped and moaned and clung to him, begging him to continue. He forced himself to hold back until she had stilled and only then did he allow himself to give in to the building explosion of desire.

Daphne knew that it was best to act as casual as possible, but she wasn't sure how to accomplish the task, given what had just happened. She felt as if Murat had somehow touched every cell in her body and made it scream with pleasure. Still, as he rolled onto his back and drew her close so she could rest her head on his shoulder, she was determined not to gush. He hardly needed the increase in his already impressive ego.

"You are amazing," he said as he stroked her bare back.

"Thank you. I could say the same thing about you."

"As you should."

She laughed. "How like a crown prince to insist on defining the compliments."

"You are made for pleasure."

"I don't know about that, but I don't mind giving in to it from time to time." Especially to a man as skilled as he. He sure knew his way around the female anatomy. Did princes get classes in that sort of thing so they didn't embarrass themselves? Were there—

"You are not a virgin."

The unexpected statement nearly didn't register. Daphne pushed herself up on one elbow and stared at him.

"Excuse me?"

"You are not a virgin."

She laughed. "Murat, I'm thirty. What did you think?"

"That you would not give yourself away so easily."

Her warm, fuzzy feelings began to fade. "You're judging me?"

He put his free hand behind his head and regarded her thoughtfully. "Even though we were engaged ten years ago, I never touched you. You left here as innocent as you arrived."

"So?"

"So tell me the name of the man who has defiled you, and I will have him tortured and beheaded."

She started to laugh, then realized he wasn't kidding. There was some definite rage bubbling under the surface.

She sat up and stared at him. "Wait a minute. You're serious."

"Deadly so."

"That's crazy. You can't kill every man I've slept with."

He frowned. "How many have there been?"

"How many women have you slept with in the past ten years?"

"That is not your concern."

"My answer exactly."

"Your situation is completely different. You are a woman. Men took advantage of you. Tell me who they are."

"You belong in the Dark Ages," she said as she scrambled to her feet and grabbed for her panties. She pulled them on, then found her bra and put that on as well.

"You're also making me crazy," she continued as she glared down at him. "I am a modern woman and have lived a relatively quiet life. Yes, there have been a few men, but I was careful about whom I chose, and no one ever took advantage of me." She threw up her hands. "Why am I explaining myself to you?"

"Because you feel bad about what happened."

"I didn't before, but I'm starting to now."

"I don't mean here," he said as he sat up. "Those other men…"

"Are none of your business." She stepped into her jeans. "You're acting like an idiot. Worse, you're acting like a sexist pig and that's even more unforgivable."

"I care about you. I want to look after you."

She picked up her shirt and slipped into it. "I don't need looking after. I've been fine for years. As for the men I slept with, I will never tell you their names. I don't want or need your protection."

Murat stood. She hated how good he looked naked and the way her body responded. Get a grip, she told herself. He was nothing but trouble. Stupid, sexist trouble. To think she'd actually been attracted to him!

While he collected his clothes, she pulled on her socks and boots.

"You're even worse than I thought," she said when she'd finished. "I don't care how good the sex is, I wouldn't marry you if the entire fate of the human race depended on it. There is nothing you can ever say or do to get me to change my mind."

He paused in the act of shrugging into his shirt. "I am Crown Prince Murat of—"

"You know what? I've heard the speech dozens of times and I'm not impressed. Not by it or you." She glared at him. "You want to know why I left you ten years ago? It's because you couldn't see past who you were enough to notice me. You didn't love me. You barely cared about me. I was just one more item on your royal to-do list. 'Get married and produce heirs.' Here's a news flash, Your Highness. A woman needs to matter to the man she marries. She needs to be with someone who needs her. I wasn't interested in marrying a man who thought of me as a mere woman."

She spied her hat and quickly scooped it up. "I left because you're just not good enough for me."

Murat could not believe what Daphne had just said. How dare she say such things to him? But before he could voice his outrage, she walked away toward the horses, collected her mount and quickly swung into the saddle. When he realized she intended to ride off without him, he grabbed his boots.

"Stop. You don't know the way."

She didn't bother answering or even looking back. Instead she gave the animal its head and took off at a canter.

"Damn her stubbornness," he muttered as he quickly pulled on his boots.

Still buttoning his shirt, he hurried to his horse and went after her.

But her head start and her mount's speed meant it would be several minutes before Murat could catch up with her. By then she had already turned toward the east and the rocky part of the desert.

"Do not go there," Murat yelled into the wind. "Stay on the path."

But Daphne either could not hear or chose not to listen. Instead of staying on the marked dirt road cut into the desert, she headed directly toward the stables in what she most likely thought would be a quicker route back.

His heart rate increased, and it had nothing to do with the speed of his horse. Instead he watched and worried until fear turned to horror as Daphne's horse came to a sudden stop and she went flying over its head and landed heavily on the hard, stony ground.

Chapter Eight

Murat lived an eternity in hell, with time crawling as he raced toward Daphne. He fumbled for his security beacon and pressed it in rapid, frantic movements, signaling an emergency. It seemed that days passed, weeks, until he could vault off his horse and crouch down beside her.

Daphne lay on the rocky ground, her legs bent beneath her, her arm thrown over her face.

He lowered it gently, then sucked in a breath as he saw her still, pale face and the pool of blood on the ground.

"No," he said to whomever would listen. "You will be fine. You must be fine."

But she did not respond, and when he touched her cheek, her skin felt cold.

Pain filled him, and fury. That such a simple mistake could cause so much damage. Then he shook off all emotion and quickly went to work examining her.

The only external bleeding came from her head and it had already begun to slow. He could not assess internal injuries but her pulse was steady and strong. If only she would awaken and start yelling at him again. If only...

The distant sound of a helicopter cut through the silence of the desert. Murat rose and waved it in, shielding her with his body when the blades kicked up dust and sand.

"She is injured," he yelled to his men. "I cannot tell how badly. We'll have to be careful of her neck and spine."

He waited until the men brought out the emergency equipment and went to work securing her before calling the stable and telling them about his horse and hers. His stallion was trained not to wander far, but her mount could be halfway to El Bahar by now.

When she had been carried into the helicopter, he joined her and took her hand in his.

"I command you to be healed," he murmured, his face close to hers, his breath stirring her hair. "I am Crown Prince Murat, and I command that you open your eyes and speak to me right now."

Nothing happened. Murat swallowed hard, then pressed his lips to her cheek. "Daphne, *please.*"

* * *

Murat paced the length of the main room in the harem. In the bedroom his personal physician reconfirmed what the doctors at the emergency room had told him. Murat tried to find a measure of peace in the knowledge that there were no internal injuries, no broken bones.

"She was very lucky," his father said from his place on the sofa. "I never thought of Daphne as a foolish young woman. To go riding off like that. You must have annoyed her."

Murat continued to watch the bedroom door. "I do so on a regular basis. It is one of my great talents." Only this time it had had too great a price.

Never again, he thought. He would not permit her to act so hastily. Left on her own, she could seriously hurt herself.

"I will stay while the doctor examines her if you wish to shower and change," the king said.

"No," Murat said immediately, then drew in a breath. "Thank you, Father, but I will stay. She is my fiancée, my responsibility."

"I see."

He doubted the king saw much, and nothing of consequence. This was Daphne. She could not be permitted to die.

At last his doctor appeared. The older man smiled.

"Good news," he said as he crossed to Murat. "It is as the other doctors told you. She has a mild concussion and some slight trauma to the brain. She will stay unconscious for a few hours, maybe a day. Then she should awaken and begin the recovery process. Within a week she will be as good as new."

"Is she in pain?" he asked.

"Not now, but when she wakes she will have a bad headache. I've left some medication to help with that. Once she's awake, keep her in bed for a couple of days, then she should take it easy for the rest of the week. I, of course, will be back in the morning and each day until she is fit again."

Murat nodded. "Thank you."

The doctor touched his arm. "Your fiancée will live to give you many healthy children, Your Highness. Fear not."

Murat heard the words, but he could not let the fear go. Not until she opened her eyes and started calling him names again.

He concluded his business with the doctor, wrote down the rest of the instructions, then hurried into the bedroom. Daphne lay in the center of the bed, hooked up to several monitors. A nurse sat in the corner. The king followed.

When Murat nodded at the nurse, she stood and quickly retreated to the living room.

"Daphne will be fine," his father said. "You heard the doctor. A nurse will be here twenty-four hours a day until she wakes up."

"No." Murat moved closer to the bed and reached for Daphne's hand. "I will be here. The nurse can wait in the living room in case there is an emergency. But until she wakes, I will tend to her."

"Murat."

He glared at his father. "No one but me."

The king nodded slowly. "As you wish."

There was only one wish, Murat thought grimly. That Daphne open her eyes.

Now, he willed her. *Look at me now.* But she slept on, unaware of his command. Even in illness she defied him. Pray God she lived to defy him another day.

Daphne felt as if someone was banging on her head with a frying pan. She remembered a frat party she'd gone to years ago while she'd been in college. She generally avoided loud parties with alcohol, but fresh from her broken engagement, she felt the need to participate in something fun and mind numbing.

So she'd gone with a couple of girlfriends and had stayed up way too late and had had too much spiked punch. In the morning she'd found herself with the mother of all hangovers and had basically wanted to die.

This was worse.

She struggled through what felt like miles of thick, sticky water, before finally surfacing. She felt bruised and sore everywhere, but it was her head that got her attention the most. Even her eyebrows hurt.

She was also, she realized, starving and in bed. The thing was, she didn't remember going to bed. She didn't remember much of anything except...

The horses. She'd been riding. She'd been angry at Murat and she'd gone on ahead, determined not to speak to him again, and then she'd been flying through the air and falling and falling and...

She opened her eyes to find herself back in the bedroom she'd been using in the harem. The walls were familiar, as was the furniture. Lamps illuminated the large space.

She glanced around, relaxing as the rest of her memory returned, only to stiffen when she saw a strange man dozing in a chair next to her bed.

He was big—tall and powerful—she could tell that even while he slept. But his hair was mussed and dark stubble darkened his jaw.

A quick glance at the clock told her the time was two. The lamplight made her think it was probably two in the morning, and turning her head increased the pounding to the point of being unbearable.

She sagged back against the pillow and studied the man. In a matter of seconds she recognized the shape of his firm jaw and mouth, the breadth of his shoulders.

"Murat?" she whispered.

Was it possible? In all the time she'd known him, both ten years ago and present day, she had never seen him anything but perfectly groomed. Why did he look so mussed, and why did he sleep in a chair beside her bed?

One of his hands lay on the blanket. She reached out and rested her fingers against his palm.

He woke instantly and glanced at her. His eyes widened.

"Daphne?"

"Hey."

He leaned forward and studied her anxiously. "How do you feel? Your head will hurt—the doctor warned me about that. I have medication for you. And if you're hungry, you can eat, but only lightly for the first day or so. You are not to get up, either. I know you can be stubborn, but I insist you follow the doctor's orders. Rest for two days, then you may begin to resume your normal activities through the end of the week. I will not accept any arguments on this matter."

Despite her aching head, she couldn't help smiling. "Of course you won't. Because this is all about you, right?"

He took her hand in both of his and kissed her fingers. "No. It is about you getting well."

His tenderness made her want to cry, which only went to show that her head injury had affected her brain.

She squeezed his hand. "How long have I been out?"

"Thirty five hours and—" he glanced at the clock "—eight minutes."

"Wow. What happened?"

"You were thrown from your horse."

"I remember that." She reached up with her free hand and gingerly touched the raised bump on her scalp. "I guess I fell headfirst."

"You did. I was concerned you had hurt yourself elsewhere, but you are fine. No broken bones, no internal injuries."

She returned her attention to him, then pulled her hand free and rubbed his cheek. The thick whiskers there grated against her skin.

"You look terrible."

He smiled. "For a good cause."

She studied his shirt and pants. "You were wearing those clothes when we went riding."

"Yes."

"You haven't showered or shaved since?"

"I wanted to be with you."

She blinked. "I don't understand."

"I have been here, with you, since we returned from the hospital."

Her head felt as if it might explode, yet she didn't feel disconnected from the conversation. Which meant she should understand what Murat was saying.

"In that chair?" she asked, trying not to sound incredulous.

"Yes."

"Beside me."

"Yes."

"Because you were…"

"Worried."

He kissed her fingers again.

Something warm and bright blossomed in her chest. Murat didn't have to stay here to watch over her. She was in his palace and completely safe. He could have an entire hospital medical team at his disposal and yet he'd stayed with her himself.

"I don't know what to say," she admitted.

"Then do not speak. There is a nurse in the other room. Let me call her to bring you the medication for your headache."

Her stomach growled.

He smiled again. "And perhaps some soup."

He rose and crossed to the doorway. As she watched him go, Daphne had to admit that she might

have been a little hasty in her judgment of Murat.
Sure he acted all in charge and "my way or the highway" but his actions told her something far different
and far more important.

He *cared* about her. When he thought she might be
in danger, he stayed by her side. What about his meetings? His princely duties? Had he neglected them all
while she'd been out of it?

She relaxed back against the pillow and sighed. She'd
been so busy resisting his demands that she'd never
taken the time to get to know the man inside. Maybe it
was time to change that. Maybe—

The nurse appeared in the doorway. She listened
while Murat spoke, nodded and left. Seconds later she
reappeared with a small plastic container in her hands.

"Take two," she said. "I will order the soup."

Murat carried the medicine over to the bed, then
helped Daphne into a sitting position. She felt her head
swim, but forced herself to stay upright long enough to
swallow the pills. He eased her back onto the bed.

"You will feel better soon," he told her.

"Thank you."

He resumed his seat and took her hand again. "My
father was here for a time. He, too, was worried."

"That was very nice of him."

The nurse walked back into the room. "I have ordered a light meal," she said. "It will be here in about ten
minutes."

Daphne winced. "I just realized the time. You had to
wake someone, didn't you?"

NO POSTAGE
NECESSARY
IF MAILED
IN THE
UNITED STATES

BUSINESS REPLY MAIL
FIRST-CLASS MAIL   PERMIT NO. 717-003   BUFFALO, NY

POSTAGE WILL BE PAID BY ADDRESSEE

SILHOUETTE READER SERVICE
3010 WALDEN AVE
PO BOX 1867
BUFFALO NY 14240-9952

Do You Have the LUCKY KEY?

PLAY THE *Lucky Key Game* **and you can get**

Scratch the gold areas with a coin. Then check below to see the books and gift you can get!

FREE BOOKS and a FREE GIFT!

YES! I have scratched off the gold areas. Please send me the **2 FREE BOOKS** and **GIFT** for which I qualify. I understand I am under no obligation to purchase any books, as explained on the back of this card.

335 SDL D39V   235 SDL D4AD

FIRST NAME	LAST NAME

ADDRESS

APT.#	CITY

STATE/PROV.	ZIP/POSTAL CODE

2 free books plus a free gift   1 free book

2 free books   Try Again!

DETACH AND MAIL CARD TODAY!

(S-SE-02/05)   ® trademarks owned and used by the trademark owner and/or its licensee.

The nurse, an attractive woman in her late forties, only smiled. "The staff was delighted to hear you are awake, Your Highness. No one minded the late hour."

"You're very kind, but—" Daphne froze as her mind replayed the woman's words. "I'm sorry. What did you call me?"

The nurse frowned slightly. "Your Highness." She glanced at Murat. "I was sure that was the right address. Am I incorrect, sir?"

He shook his head. "You did well. Now if you would please go wait for the meal?"

"Of course."

The woman left.

Daphne stared after her. A thousand thoughts bombarded her bruised brain and made it impossible for her to think clearly.

Something was wrong. Very wrong.

"Murat," she began.

"Do not trouble yourself," he told her. "All will be well."

She wasn't about to be put off. Not now. "She called me Your Highness, and you said that was correct."

"It is."

Panic flooded her. She struggled to sit up, but he pressed down on her shoulders.

"You must rest," he said.

"I must know the truth." She glared at him, willing herself to be wrong. Completely and totally wrong. "Why did she call me that?"

He picked up her left hand and fingered the diamond band on her ring finger. A diamond ring she'd never seen before in her life.

"Because you are now my wife."

Chapter Nine

Daphne wanted to shriek loudly enough to cause the ancient stone walls to crack. She wanted oceans to rise up, and thunder to shake the heavens. But she knew if she opened her mouth and really let loose, all she would have to show for it was a worsening of her already pounding headache.

Murat was speaking a foreign language, she told herself in an effort to stay calm, or he was the one with the head injury. Except, she knew neither was true and that this was all real, yet how was it possible?

"You married me while I was unconscious?" she demanded in a voice that was perilously close to shrieky.

"You need to stay calm."

"I need to have you killed," she said, narrowing her eyes, then wishing she hadn't when the pain increased. "What is wrong with you? You can't do that sort of thing. It's horrible and it's illegal."

"Not technically."

Murat continued to rub her fingers. When she realized that, she pulled them free.

"In a Bahanian royal marriage, the bride does not have to agree," he continued. "She merely has to not disagree."

"Silence as consent?" she asked, unable to believe this.

"Yes."

"Did anyone notice that I wasn't in a position to agree *or* disagree? I was *unconscious* with a head injury?"

He shrugged. "It was a matter of discussion."

"That's it? No one protested?"

"No."

Of course not. Because who would? Certainly not Murat and— "Who else was there?"

"The man who officiated and the king."

"That's it? No other witnesses?"

He smiled. "The king is enough of a witness."

She couldn't believe Murat's father had been in on this. Her head continued to throb, and now she felt tears burning in her eyes.

Don't cry, she told herself. Crying would only make her weak, and she had to stay strong, but it was hard. All she wanted to do was curl up in a ball and sob her heart out.

"You can't do this," she said.

"It is already done."

"Then I'll undo it. I'll get an annulment or a divorce. I don't care about the scandal."

"The king must give his permission for the union of a crown prince to be dissolved."

Which meant when pigs fly, what with the monarch being in on the sleazy ceremony.

"You're a lying weasel bastard with the morals of a pack of wild dogs," she said angrily. "I'll never forgive you for this. Mark my words. I *will* find a way out of this."

He had the nerve to brush her hair off her face. "Rest now, Daphne. You can deal with our marriage in a few days."

She smacked his hand away. "Don't touch me. Not ever again. I hate you."

That got his attention. Murat straightened, then stood and walked to the foot of the bed where he loomed over her.

"You forget yourself."

"Not even for a second. If I'm your *wife*—" the word tasted bitter on her tongue "—then I can do as I please."

"You will still remember your place."

"Oh, right. That would be as your slave here in the harem. Gee, how exciting. I'm delighted to be the unimportant plaything of a dictatorial, arrogant, selfish prince."

He glowered at her.

She didn't care about anything he might be thinking.

And the pill must be kicking in because the pain started to fade.

She pushed herself into a sitting position and glared back at him with all her considerable fury.

"You are a most frustrating woman," he said.

"Let me tell you how much I don't care about your opinion."

He drew his eyebrows together. "You complain now, but I did this for you."

"Oh, right. Because I've been begging for us to be married."

"No, because of what happened. You hurt yourself. Someone has to watch over you."

"You married me to protect me from myself?" She didn't dare shake her head in disbelief, although she wanted to. "I guess you're reduced to telling yourself lies so you can sleep at night."

To think that she'd gotten all soft and gooey inside thinking he actually cared about her, that he'd worried while she'd been out of it. Instead he'd simply been protecting his new toy.

"There is also the fact that we made love," he said, as if explaining things to a small and slow child. "You were not a virgin."

What on earth did that have to do with anything? "So?"

"You should have been."

"You married me to punish me?"

"Of course not." The glower returned. "You are being most difficult."

"Gee, I wonder why. So you're saying you married

me because I wasn't a virgin, but if I had been we would have been flirting with defiling territory, so that wouldn't have been much better."

"You are correct. I would have married you if you had been a virgin."

Talk about being between a rock and a hard place.

The sensation of being trapped sucked the last of her energy. Daphne slid down onto the mattress and closed her eyes.

"You are feeling unwell?" he asked.

"Go away."

She heard him walk closer, then he touched her forehead. "I wish to help."

She forced herself to open her eyes and stare at him. "Do you think I will ever care about what you want? Get out now. I never want to see you again. Get out. Get out!"

She screamed as loudly as she could. When Murat still hesitated, she reached for the empty glass on her nightstand and picked it up to use as a weapon.

"Get out!"

"I will check on you in the morning."

"Get out!"

He turned and left.

She put down the glass, then curled up in the big bed and closed her eyes. The pain was still with her, but this one had nothing to do with her head injury and everything to do with the loss of her freedom.

She didn't doubt that Murat had married her and that she was well and truly caught in circumstances that would be difficult to undo. The sense of betrayal hurt more than anything. Her eyes began to burn again, but this time she didn't fight the tears. She gave in to them, even though she knew they wouldn't help in the least.

With the aid of the painkillers, Daphne managed to sleep through the night. She saw the doctor the next morning, who told her to stay in bed at least twenty-four more hours and not to return to her normal routine for a few days.

For reasons she didn't understand but was grateful for, Murat didn't return to visit her, which meant she was left in solitude, except for the quiet presence of the nurse who brought her meals and stayed out of her way.

On day three, Daphne sent the poor woman away. "I'm fine," she said after she'd showered and dressed and found that walking wasn't all that difficult. "You should return to someone who actually needs your help."

"You're very kind, Your Highness," the woman said. "I wish you and the crown prince a long and happy marriage."

Daphne didn't know what to say, so she smiled and thanked her again. Obviously, she'd been out of the room when Daphne'd had her screaming fit. No one witnessing that could ever imagine a successful relationship as the outcome.

She still had bouts of weariness and despair, but when they hit, she used her anger to fuel herself. Murat wasn't going to get away with this. She wasn't sure what she was going to have to do to get away, but she would find out and make it happen.

After finishing her breakfast, she walked to the gold doors and pulled them open. No guards. No doubt Murat had released them from their duties after the wedding. He no longer had to worry about her escaping. As the queen, she couldn't go out unaccompanied. No driver would take her. No pilot would leave the country without express permission. She might have the freedom of the palace now, but that simply meant she'd graduated to a larger prison.

She walked through the quiet halls of the palace. As always the beauty of the structure pleased her. She paused to admire a particularly lovely and detailed tapestry of several children in a garden. She recognized the stone wall and the placement of several trees. The scene might be from four hundred years ago, but the garden itself still existed just outside.

The history of Bahania called to her, but she ignored the whispers. There was nothing anyone could say or do to convince her she had to make her peace with what had happened.

She saw several people hurrying from place to place. When she recognized one of the senior staff, she stopped the man and asked after the king. The man led her outside, and Daphne stepped into bright sunshine.

For a second the light hurt her eyes and made her head throb, but she adjusted, then made her way along the stone path. She heard voices before she saw the people, and when she turned the corner, she recognized Cleo, Sadik's wife, with the king.

They sat across from each other. A pretty baby stood between them.

"You are so very clever," the king said with obvious delight. "Come to Grandpa. You can do it."

The baby, dressed in pink from the bows in her fine hair down to the hearts on her tiny laces, laughed and toddled toward the king. He caught her and swept her up in the air.

"Ah, Calah, I had not thought to find love at this stage in my life, but you have truly stolen my heart." He kissed her cheek.

Cleo grinned. "I'll bet you say that to all the grandkids."

"Of course. Because it is true."

Daphne didn't know what to do. While she had business with the king, she didn't want to interrupt such a private family moment. She felt a twinge of longing for the connection the king had with his daughter-in-law. Cleo might have come from ordinary circumstances, but no one held that against her. Funny how a girl who grew up in foster care and worked in a copy shop could go on to marry a prince and be accepted by all involved, while Daphne had never been as welcome in her own family.

King Hassan looked up and saw her. "Daphne. You are looking well. Come." He patted the bench. "Join us."

She moved forward and greeted Cleo and her daughter. "She's walking," she said, touching Calah's plump cheek and smiling.

The baby gurgled back.

"Barely," Cleo said. "Which is okay with me. She's a complete terror when she crawls. I can only imagine what will happen when she starts running everywhere.

I'm going to have to get one of those herding dogs to keep her out of trouble."

The king shook his head. "You will dote on her as you always do. As will Sadik."

"Probably." Cleo bent down and collected Calah. "But right now we have to deal with a dirty diaper. See you later."

Her exit was so quick and graceful, Daphne wondered if it had been planned in advance. Not that anyone would tell her. She seemed to be the last to know about almost everything.

"How are you?" the king asked as he turned toward Daphne and took one of her hands in his.

The right one, she noticed. Not the left one, now bare of the ring Murat had given her. She'd left that in her rooms.

"I'm feeling better physically," she said. "Emotionally I'm still in a turmoil." She stared directly at the king. "Is he telling the truth? Did Murat really marry me while I was unconscious?"

"Yes, he did."

It was as if all the air rushed out of her lungs. For a second she thought she might pass out.

"Are you all right?" King Hassan asked.

"Yes. I just…" Her last hope died. "I don't understand why you allowed this to happen. What Murat did was wrong."

"The crown prince cannot *be* wrong."

Ah, so they were going to close ranks around her. "I don't believe that, and I don't think you believe it, either. He had no right to trap me into a marriage I don't want. Neither of us will ever be happy. Surely you want more for your son."

"I am confident you can work things out."

She stared in the king's handsome face. He was so much like his son—stubborn, determined to get his own way, and he held all the cards.

"I want an annulment," she said quietly.

He patted the back of her hand. "Let us not speak of that. Instead, we will talk of the beauty of Bahania. If I remember correctly you enjoyed your time here. Now you will be able to explore the wonders of our country. You can meet the people. I understand you have become a veterinarian. Practicing your chosen profession outside of the palace could present a problem, but we can work on that. Perhaps you could do some teaching. Also, I have enough cats to keep you busy."

She felt as if she were sitting next to a wall. Nothing was getting through.

"Your Majesty, please. You have to help me."

He smiled. "Daphne, I believe there is a reason you never married. It has been ten years since you left Bahania. Why, in all that time, did no other man claim your heart?"

"I never met the right man. I've been busy with my career and—" She stared at him. "It's not because I've been pining for Murat."

"So you say. He tells me much the same. But he never found anyone, either. Now you are together, as it was always meant to be."

This wasn't happening. "He trapped me. Tricked me. How can you approve of that?"

"Give it time. Get to know him. I think you'll be happy with what you find."

The hopelessness of the situation propelled her to her feet. "If you'll excuse me," she mumbled before turning and hurrying back toward the side door into the palace.

She felt broken from the inside out. No one would listen; no one would help. The tangled web of her circumstances would tug at her until she gave in and surrendered.

"Never," she breathed. "I'll be strong."

She turned a corner and nearly ran into a young woman in a maid's uniform.

"Oh, Your Highness. I was sent to look for you." The woman smiled. "Your parents have called and wish to speak with you. If you will please follow me."

No doubt her parents had learned about the marriage. They wouldn't care about the circumstances, she thought glumly.

Sure enough, when she picked up the phone, her mother couldn't stop gushing.

"It's wonderful," she said. "We're thrilled."

Her father had picked up the extension. "You did good, baby girl."

Tears burned in Daphne's eyes. Funny how until this moment, she'd never heard those words from her father before. Apparently she'd never "done good" until she'd been trapped in marriage to a man she didn't love.

Her mother sniffed. "We would have liked a big wedding, but this is fine, too. I read that there will be a huge reception in a few months, so as soon as you have the dates, let us know. We'll need to make arrangements to fly over. Oh, darling, I'm so happy for you. Are you happy? Isn't this fabulous? And just think—in a year or so, we'll hear the pitter patter of a little prince or princess. Oh, Daphne. You've made us so proud."

Her mother kept on talking while her father added his few comments, but Daphne wasn't listening anymore. Instead she stared blankly out a window as a horrible, stomach-dropping thought occurred to her.

She and Murat had made love without protection. Right there in the oasis, she'd let him take her to paradise and back never once considering the consequences. She could be pregnant.

"I have to go," she said, and listened as they told her of course they understood. A woman in her position had responsibilities and they would talk soon.

She hung up and tried to shake off her daze.

Pregnant. Oh, God. If that was true… She knew enough about Bahanian law to know that no royal child was ever allowed to leave the country in the case of a divorce. Which meant if she had a baby, she would be forced to stay here forever. Abandoning her child wasn't an option.

"It was just one time," she told herself as she hurried back to the harem. She couldn't get pregnant that easily, could she?

As she stepped off the elevator, she saw another

young woman in a maid's uniform sitting in a straight-back chair by the gold harem doors. When the woman saw her, she rose.

"Your Highness, I was asked to wait until you returned. It is my honor to show you to your new quarters."

Daphne's headache had returned. "New quarters?" Oh. "With the crown prince."

The young woman beamed. "Yes. If you will follow me."

She didn't want to. She wanted to sit down right there and never move again.

"My things?" she asked.

"Have been sent ahead."

Of course. Murat would want the details taken care of so she couldn't put up a fuss.

"Very well," she said, wanting only to find a quiet place and close her eyes until the pain went away. Not just the pain from her head, either, but the aching in her heart.

She allowed the woman to lead her to the elevator, then through a maze of hallways, with them finally stopping in front of a large, carved wooden door. The maid opened it and Daphne stepped inside.

Her first impression was of openness and light. Massive windows and French doors led onto a private balcony with what seemed to be a view of the world. It was only after she'd stared at the vastness of the city and the water did she realize they were at the very top of the palace, on the corner.

To the left was the Arabian Sea, twinkling blue and teal and green in the sunlight. To the right was the skyline of the city. And beyond it all, the desert stretched for miles, compelling in its starkness.

When she returned her attention from the view to the room, she saw comfortable furniture, an impressive collection of artwork and a space big enough to roller blade in. Doors led to other rooms. Most likely a dining area, a bedroom and an office, in case the crown prince wanted to work from "home." Because she had no doubt she had been brought to Murat's suite of rooms. Where else would his wife live?

Her heart ached, her legs felt as if they would give way at any moment and her head throbbed. She thanked the maid and made her way to what she hoped was the bedroom. Unfortunately, when she stepped inside, she found she was not alone.

Murat sat in a chair in the corner. Waiting? She wasn't sure. She ignored him as she made her way to the huge bed and crawled onto the mattress.

"You are ill," he said as he jumped to his feet. "I will call the doctor."

"I'm fine," she told him. "Just tired. Please, leave me alone."

"I cannot."

She turned away, curling up on the embroidered bedspread and doing her best not to give in to the tears. Not again. There had been too many over the past few days.

But the strain was too much and the first tear leaked out of the corner of her eye. She did her best to hide it, but somehow Murat knew. He sat on the bed and gathered her in his arms.

"It is all right," he said quietly.

"No. It's not and you're the reason."

He stroked her hair and her back and rocked her. She wanted to protest that she wasn't a child, that he couldn't make things better with a kiss and a hug, but speaking was too difficult. Right now it was all she could do to breathe.

She wasn't sure how long he held her, but eventually the pain eased. The tears dried up, and when he offered her his handkerchief, she took it and blew her nose.

"I talked to your father," she said. "He won't help me."

"Are you surprised?"

"More like disappointed." She shifted away from him and stared in his face. "You know I will never forgive you for this."

Murat did know. Marrying Daphne that way had been a calculated risk. But once he had made up his mind, there was no going back. He would face her wrath in the short term to gain her acceptance in the long term.

"Time is a great healer," he said.

"Not in this case. My anger will only grow."

He tucked her hair behind her ear and smiled. "I have seen the new sculpture you have started. I believe it is going to be me falling down the stairs. You have found a way to release your anger."

"It's not enough." Her blue eyes flashed fury. "You had no right to—"

He pressed his fingers against her mouth. "Let us not have that conversation again."

"Then which one do you want to have? The one

where I call you a lying bastard? The one where I say that taking away my freedom is an unforgivable act and that you'll never get away with it?"

"They are variations on a theme."

"It's what I want to talk about."

She was so beautiful, he thought. Not just in her fury, but always. There was an intensity about her, and he longed for that energy to be focused on him.

He captured her left hand and held it in his. "You do not wear your ring."

"Why would I?"

"Because it is a symbol of our marriage and your position in my world." He pulled the ring from his pocket and tried to slide it on her finger. She pulled back.

"You are not usually one to act like a child," he said.

"I'm making an exception."

"Very well. I will leave it here until you change your mind." He set the ring on the nightstand.

She drew in a breath. "I'm leaving, Murat. Eventually I'll find a way to escape you and this palace."

"You are not my prisoner."

"Of course I am. I have been from the beginning. I don't suppose you would care to tell me why."

"You have made all the choices, save one."

"Yeah, that last really big one when there was a wedding." She pressed her lips together. "I *will* leave just as soon as I'm sure I'm not pregnant."

Her words crashed into him. He stood and stared at her. "Pregnant?"

She rolled her eyes. "Don't you give me that happy

expectant-father face. It's unlikely. We only did it the one time, and let me tell you how much I'm regretting that incident."

Pregnant. Of course. He had been so caught up in making love with Daphne that he had not taken precautions, which was very unlike him. He had always been careful not to be trapped by that particular game.

A child. A son. An heir.

"Stop grinning," she demanded.

"Am I?" He felt as if he could fly.

"There's no baby."

"You don't know that."

"I'm reasonably confident. It was just one time."

"It only takes one time." He cupped her cheek. "You understand the law, Daphne. You know what happens if there is a child."

Despair entered her eyes. "You win. I couldn't leave my baby, and I would never be allowed to take him or her from the country." She shook off his touch. "But know this. I'm not sleeping with you ever again, and as soon as I know I'm not pregnant, I'm leaving."

Strong words, but he doubted she meant them. Not completely. "Would you leave the people of Bahania so soon? You are their future queen."

"They've lived without me this long. I'm sure they can survive into the future."

"You will change your mind."

"I won't." She stood and faced him. "Murat, you think this is a game, but it's very serious. I don't want to be here. I don't want to be married to you."

"I will convince you."

"You can't."

But he could. He knew that. He was Crown Prince Murat of Bahania, and she was a mere woman. Her will could not withstand the pressure of his.

He knew now he should never have let her go all those years ago. It was a mistake he would not repeat again.

"I want to love the man I marry," she told him earnestly. "I don't love you."

"You will."

"How do you figure? You're going to force me to love you?"

"Yes."

"It's not possible."

"Watch me."

Chapter Ten

Cleo sat in the middle of several boxes of shoes and grinned. "So I guess when you're the once and future queen, you don't go to the accessories, the accessories come to you."

Daphne wove her way between nearly a dozen racks of clothes sent over to the palace by boutique owners and fashion designers.

"The clothes, too," she said as she took a cashmere jacket off a rack and studied the light-blue color. "This is overwhelming."

Cleo held up a pair of strappy sandals. "I hate you for not having the same size feet as me. Just so we're all clear. I don't think I've ever seen a shoe this narrow."

"Or as long," Daphne said. "I have big feet."

"But skinny. I, of course, wear a 6 wide." She wiggled her hot-pink painted toes. "Billie's going to have a heart attack when I tell her what she's missed."

Daphne put the jacket back on the rack and returned to the sofa. "Then please don't tell her while she's flying. She only has a couple more weeks until the doctors ground her for the rest of her pregnancy. Besides, as far as I can tell, the clothesfest is going to go on for several more weeks, so she's welcome anytime."

"Cool." Cleo dropped the shoes back in the box and picked up a leather handbag. "At least I can borrow this. If you're getting it. Are you?"

"I have no idea."

The clothes had started arriving three days ago. At first Daphne had kept the racks in the spare bedroom in their suite, but that space had filled rapidly. She'd finally asked for a large unused conference area and had all the clothes brought down, along with some sofas and several large mirrors. Dressing as the wife of the crown prince was serious business.

"You should be happier," Cleo said. "These are all beautiful."

"I know." Daphne did her best to smile. She wasn't sure she'd been convincing.

The problem was without Calah around to distract her—the baby was currently down for her nap—Cleo was far too observant. Daphne didn't know what to say to her new sister-in-law. That it had been a week and she still felt angry and trapped.

True to her word, she avoided Murat as much as possible and slept in the suite's guest room. He acted as if there was nothing out of the ordinary and insisted on discussing their future in terms of decades.

"Want to talk about it?" Cleo asked.

"I don't know what there is to say." Or how much she was willing to confess.

"I know the marriage happened pretty fast," Cleo said as she stood and walked over to the same sofa and sat at the opposite end. She fingered her short, spiky blond hair. "There was some talk."

"I'll bet. It's just…" She sighed. "I didn't ask for this. I know, I know." She held up both hands. "Boo-hoo for the poor woman who married a prince and will one day be queen. How sad."

Cleo shook her head. "If you're not happy, you're not happy."

"I wish it were that simple." She didn't want to talk about what Murat had done. Somehow she guessed that Cleo wouldn't want the information, nor would she act on it.

"Have you thought about giving the relationship a chance?" Cleo asked. "I know these guys act all imperious, but underneath, they're amazing husbands. You just have to get past the barrier down to their hearts."

"I don't think Murat has a heart."

"Do you really mean that?"

"No." He must have. Somewhere. "I'm finding the situation overwhelming. I'm doing interviews later for my chief of staff. I need someone to help me stay organized. Invitations are pouring in. I don't want to accept any of them, but Murat has to go, which means…"

She still hadn't decided what it meant. Did she go with him? Put on a front and pretend to be the happy bride? Did she refuse? While she wouldn't mind rubbing his face in what he'd done, he wasn't the only one involved. In some ways she felt responsible for the citizens of Bahania. She didn't want them embarrassed by her behavior.

"I don't want to make life easier for him," she admitted, "but my own sense of what is right is on his side. I really hate that."

Cleo leaned close. "You're thinking too much. Just relax and take each day as it comes. These royal things get easier with time. At least you have the advantage of breeding. You should have seen my first few lesson with the etiquette guy. I think I completely scared him."

Daphne stared into Cleo's big blue eyes and easy smile. "I doubt that. I'm sure he was charmed."

"Not when I accidentally poured the hot tea into his lap instead of his fine china cup."

Daphne laughed. "I'll bet that got his attention."

"In more ways than one." She shrugged. "The princes are worth it. That's the best advice I can give you. Know that they're worth every annoyance, every pain. I'm so thankful I met Sadik and fell in love with him. It wasn't easy, but now…" She grinned. "I know this sounds lame, but my life is perfect."

"I'm happy for you," Daphne said, and meant it. Cleo

had grown up in difficult circumstances. She'd more than earned her happy ending.

But not everyone's story was the same. Should Daphne ignore her responsibilities because she was still intent on leaving? Should she play the part while she was here? And if she played it too much, would she become complaisant? She would never forgive herself if she gave in to Murat. Worse, she would have taught him not only was it acceptable to treat her badly, but that there were no consequences. Ignoring everything else, did she want to be married to a man who thought so little of her?

Cleo stood. "Sorry to gush over your clothing and run, but Calah will be waking up soon and I want to be there." She smiled. "Sadik tells me that our nanny has the cushiest job around. Great pay and I never let her do any work."

"Your daughter is lucky."

"I like to think I'm the lucky one." She wiggled her fingers at Daphne and crossed to the door. When she reached it, she turned back. "If you need to talk more, you know where I live."

"Absolutely."

"Good. I'll—" Cleo gave a laugh and turned around "—look who just appeared," she said and dragged Murat into the room. "Your wife needs help," she said. "Too many good clothing choices. Maybe you could talk her into modeling a few things for you."

Murat glanced between the women. "An intriguing proposition. I will consider it."

Cleo left.

Daphne stayed where she was on the sofa while Murat walked through the maze of racks and the boxes of shoes, purses and scarves.

"Have you made sense out of any of this?" he asked.

"Not really. I need a schedule first to figure out what sort of clothing I'll need."

"I see. And you do not want to agree to a schedule because that is too much like giving in."

She shrugged, even though he'd guessed correctly.

"You have time," he said. "No one will expect you to have a full schedule right away."

"And if I don't want one ever?"

He sat down across from her. "There are advantages and disadvantages to any position in life."

"I know your advantages," she said. "You pretty much get whatever you want."

"True, but there is a price to pay."

"Which is?"

"I have much to offer. Favors, knowledge, an interesting circle of acquaintances. Who comes to see me because of who I am and who comes because of what I can do for him?" He loosened his tie. "Now I am aware of the possibilities at the first meeting, but when I was younger, it was not so easy to see those who expected something in return."

Daphne understood exactly what he meant. "I had the same thing, on a much smaller scale. Not so much with friends, but sometimes my teachers were too impressed by my parents to actually pay attention to me."

"Exactly." He shrugged. "Reyhan, Sadik and Jefri were free to roam the city, making trouble, having fun. I was not. While they played, I learned about governments and rulers and history. All in preparation. Each day I was reminded of my responsibility to my people. I did not know who they all were, but sometimes I hated them."

The man sat across from her but she could easily picture the boy. Tired, restless, but forced to stay inside for one more lesson when all he wanted was to go play with his brothers.

Compassion made it difficult for her to want to keep her distance, which meant he was making good on his word to convince her to care about him. Talk about smooth.

"While we are on the subject," he said, "your father called me. He wishes to discuss expanding the family business into Bahania, and from there El Bahar and the Middle East."

Daphne couldn't believe it. Her own father? Heat flared on her cheeks and she had a bad feeling she was blushing.

"I'm sorry," she said. "I'll phone him right away."

Murat leaned back in the sofa and shook his head. "There is no need. As my father-in-law, he is due some consideration. I will put my people on it and he can work through them."

"It's only been a week," she said, angry that after years of ignoring her, her father was now willing to use her situation to his advantage. "He could have waited a little longer."

"Perhaps, but if you allow yourself to get upset over every person who comes looking for something, then you will spend your life in a state of great anxiety. It means nothing, Daphne. Let it go."

Maybe it meant nothing to him, but it meant something to her. Unfortunately, no matter how much she wanted to hate Murat, he was the only person who could understand what she was going through.

She didn't want to live in a world where people used her to get what they wanted, yet that had been his whole life.

"Have you ever been sure about anyone?" she asked. "How do you know if he or she is interested in you or what you can offer?"

"Sometimes the situation is very clear. Those are the people I prefer. When I know what they are after I can decide to give it or not. But when they play the game too well…" He sighed. "I was more easily fooled when I was younger. After college, a few women managed to convince me that their love for me was greater than the universe itself when what they really wanted was the title and money."

She winced. "That couldn't have been fun."

"No. But for every half-dozen of them there was someone sincere. A young woman who didn't know or didn't care. You, for example."

She smiled at the memory. "I didn't have a clue."

"I know, and when you found out, I thought you would run so far in the opposite direction that I would never catch you."

Her smile faded. "And when I did run, you didn't come after me."

He stared at her, then dropped his gaze to her left hand. "You still refuse to wear your ring."

"Are you surprised?"

"No. Disappointed."

"Want to talk about what I'm feeling?"

"If you would like."

She narrowed her gaze. "That's new. Since when do you care about my feelings regarding anything?"

"I want you to be happy."

She couldn't believe it. "You kept me prisoner, then married me against my will. Not exactly a recipe for happiness."

"We are husband and wife now. I would like you to make the best of the situation. You may find yourself pleasantly surprised."

She leaned toward him. "Murat, when will you see what you did was wrong? Why won't you at least admit it? I meant what I said. I want out."

"There will be no divorce. The king will not allow it."

Daphne stood, with the thought of escaping, only there wasn't anywhere to go. She glanced around at all the clothes she had to try on, the reminder about her interviews, the stack of books on history and protocol.

"Did it ever occur to you that whatever chance we might have had for happiness is now dead because of what you did?" she asked quietly.

Murat stood and moved close. He touched her cheek. "In time you will let go of the past and look toward the future. I can be patient. I will wait. In the meantime I have a meeting." He glanced at his watch. "For which I am now late."

"Somehow I don't think you'll get a reprimand."

He flashed her a smile. "Probably not." He nodded at the clothes. "Are you truly overwhelmed?"

"Of course. How could I not be?"

"Would you like to leave this all behind for a few days?"

"Is that possible?"

"Yes. Although it requires you getting back on a horse."

"I can do that."

"Good." He tightened his tie. "Be ready, tomorrow at dawn. You'll need to dress traditionally. I will have someone leave the appropriate clothing in our room."

"Where are we going?"

"It's a surprise."

Daphne spent a restless night in the small guest-room bed. She couldn't stop thinking about Murat, which wasn't all that uncommon, only this time she wasn't nearly so angry.

Maybe it was because they'd discussed a little of his past. She wouldn't have enjoyed being hampered by so many restrictions. While it might be good to be the king, growing up as the prince sounded less fun.

She appreciated his understanding of what her father had done, but hated that such things were common-place to him. Who had ever cared about Murat simply for himself? Who had ever loved him?

She didn't mean family, but someone else. A woman. Had there been even one to care about the man more than the position he held?

She opened her eyes and stared into the darkness. Would she have? Ten years ago, if she hadn't run, would she have loved him more than anyone?

Of course, she thought. She already had. She'd wanted to get lost in him and have him get lost in her. She hadn't run because of her feelings, but because of a lack of his. At twenty, she'd needed to be important, an emotional equal. She'd wanted to matter.

Funny how ten years later her goal hadn't changed.

That's what he didn't understand. Of course she was furious about how he'd forced her into marriage. He was wrong and egotistical and he deserved some kind of punishment. But if he'd come to her and even hinted that she mattered, she might have been willing to accept his apology and give things a try. Not that Murat would ever admit he'd done anything wrong, let alone apologize.

While it was her nature to make the best of a bad situation, she believed down to her bones that he had to understand he'd acted selfishly.

She rose and turned off the alarm, then moved into the small bathroom to shower. Every night Murat invited her to share the large, luxurious bedroom and every night she refused. Now, as she stood under the spray of hot water, she found her body remembering what it had been like to make love with him. She wanted to feel his touch again.

"Which only goes to show you're in need of some

serious therapy," she muttered as she turned away from the spray.

After drying herself and her hair and applying plenty of lotion to combat the dryness of the desert, she slipped on her bra and panties, then a lightweight T-shirt and jeans. Next came her riding boots, followed by the traditional robes that covered her from shoulder to toes. Last, she slipped on her head covering.

As she stared at herself in the mirror, the only part of her she recognized was her blue eyes. Otherwise, she could have been any other Bahanian woman of the desert. Most women who lived in the city had long abandoned the traditional dress, but she and Murat would be heading into the desert where the old ways were still favored.

She left the bedroom and found Murat waiting for her in the living room.

He wore a loose-fitting white shirt and riding pants. She could see her reflection in his boots.

"I can arrange a Jeep if you would prefer," he said by way of greeting.

"I'd rather ride. I won't go off by myself again. I've learned my lesson."

He nodded, then held out his hand. The diamond wedding band rested on it. "We are married. I will not have my people asking questions."

She stared at the ring, then at him. The internal battle was a short one because she agreed that she did not want others brought into their private battle of wills. She took the ring and slipped it on.

His expression didn't change at all. She'd half expected him to gloat and was pleased when he didn't.

"Shall we go?" he asked.

Murat stepped out of the car into the milling crowd by the stable. Nearly fifty people collected supplies, checked horses, loaded trucks or called out names on the master list. His head of security gave him a thumbs-up, before returning to the conversation he'd been having with his team.

Murat helped Daphne out of the car, then waited while she glanced around.

"Did you say something about roughing it?" she asked in amusement. "I was picturing us on a couple of horses, with a camel carrying a few supplies."

"This is not much more than that."

She laughed. "Of course not. You do know how to travel in style."

"Will you feel better knowing we are to sleep in a tent?"

"Gee, how big will it be?"

"Not large. A few thousand square feet."

"However will we survive?"

"Everyone else is housed elsewhere. There is a kitchen tent, a communication tent and so on."

She shaded her eyes as she stared into the distance. "I'm glad we're going."

As was he. Even shrouded in yards of fabric, she was still beautiful. He had not enjoyed the past week—her anger and silence. He hated that she slept in another bed, although he would not force her into his.

Why did she not understand that what was done was done and now they should get on with their lives? Did she really think that being married to him was such a hardship? She insulted him with her reluctance and sad eyes.

"Daphne," he said, drawing her attention back to him. "About our time in the desert. I would like us to call a truce."

"I'm not sure that's possible when only one of us is fighting," she said. "But I understand what you're saying."

She looked at the horses, then the camels and trucks. "Will we be joined by some of the nomadic tribes?"

"Yes. Word has spread that I will be among my people. They will join us as they can."

She looked back at him. "I agree to the truce, but for your people, not for you."

"As you wish."

For now it was enough. If she spent time with him and forgot to be angry, he knew he could win her over. Then when they returned to the palace, all would be well.

"Come," he said, holding out his hand.

She took it and allowed him to lead her to a snow-white gelding.

"Try not to fall off this one," he said as he helped her mount.

She settled into the saddle and grinned down at him. "Try not to make me angry."

"That is never my goal."

"But you're so good at it."

"I am a man of many talents."

Something flashed in her eyes. Something dark and

sensuous that heated his blood and increased his ever-present wanting.

"We're not going there," she said. "Don't think for a moment there's going to be any funny business."

"But you enjoy laughing."

"That's not what I mean and you know it."

"So many rules."

"I mean this one."

"As you wish."

She might mean it but that did not prevent him from changing her mind. The desert was often a place of romance and he intended to use the situation to his advantage. Their tent might be large and well furnished, but there was only one bedroom…and one bed.

"Tell me where we're going," Daphne said after they'd been traveling for about an hour. "Is it a specific route? We're on a road." Sort of. More of a dirt track that cut through the desert.

"Yes. This leads north to the ancient Silk Road. We will not go that far—just into the heart of the desert."

The Silk Road. She'd heard of it, studied it. To think they were so close. There was so much history in Bahania. So many treasures for her to discover.

She shifted slightly in her saddle. After a few minutes of trepidation after finding herself back on a horse, she'd quickly settled into the rhythmic striding and lost her fear. Murat riding close beside her helped.

She supposed it wasn't a good sign that the very man

who made her insane also made her feel safe. "Will we be camping by an oasis?" she asked.

"Each night. Eventually we will make our way to—" He hesitated.

"What?" she asked.

"We are going to a place of great mystery. It is not far out of our way, and I thought you would enjoy reacquainting yourself with my sister Sabrina."

Daphne remembered the pretty, intelligent teenager from her previous visit to Bahania. "She lives out here?"

"Yes, with her husband. My sister Zara resides there, as well."

"Zara. Okay, she's the daughter of the dancer. The American who found out she was the king's daughter a few years ago?"

"Exactly. She is married to an American sheik named Rafe. He is the chief of security."

"Of what?"

Murat looked at her. "That is the secret. You must take a solemn vow to never reveal it to anyone." He seemed to be perfectly serious.

"You know I'm still planning to leave," she said.

"We agreed not to speak of such things."

"Not speaking doesn't take away the truth. But I would never betray the people of Bahania. Or you."

He nodded, as if he'd expected no less. "You have heard of the City of Thieves?"

She thought for a second. "It's a myth. Like Atlantis. A beautiful city in the middle of the desert where those who steal find sanctuary. Supposedly some of the most amazing missing treasures are said to reside there. Jewels, paintings, statues, tapestries. If a country has lost something of great value in the last thousand years, it can probably be found in the City of Thieves."

"It is true."

She blinked. "Excuse me?"

"All of it. The city exists."

"You mean like a real city. Buildings. People. Cool stolen stuff?"

"There is a castle built in the twelfth century and a small city surrounding it. An underground spring provides water. The buildings all blend so perfectly with their surroundings that they cannot be seen from any distance or from the sky." He motioned to the large crowd behind them. "We will leave nearly everyone long before we near the city. Prince Kardal will send out his own security forces to escort us in."

"I can't believe it," she breathed. "It's like finding out the Easter bunny is real."

"Sabrina is an expert on the antiquities there. Due to her influence, several pieces have already been returned to some countries. She will take you on a tour if you would like."

"I'd love it. When do we get there?"

He laughed. "Not so fast. First we must ride deep into the desert and find our way to the edge of the world."

"I've never been there," she admitted, more than a little intrigued.

"It is a place worth visiting."

Chapter Eleven

Daphne might hate the way Murat had arranged their marriage and not enjoy being kept in Bahania against her will, but she had to admit that the man knew how to travel and travel well.

Small trucks with large tires kept pace with the group on horse- and camelback. Several vehicles were designated as moving cafeterias, offering everything from cold water to sandwiches and fresh fruit.

Lunch had been a hit-and-miss affair, eaten while her horse drank and rested, but Murat promised a dinner feast when they reached their camp for the first night.

He had also promised more people would join them, and he was true to his word.

By midafternoon, the number of travelers had tripled. Every hour or so another group appeared on the horizon and moved toward them. There were families with small herds of camels or goats, several young men with carts, and what looked like entire tribes.

Murat's security spoke with them first, inspected a few bags and boxes, then let them join the growing throng. A few of the men rode to the front of the queue and spoke briefly with Murat. She noticed that those brave enough to do so seemed to focus most of their attention on her.

"Why do they do that?" she asked as a man bowed low in his saddle and returned to his family somewhere behind them. "If they want to meet me, why don't they just ask?"

"It is not our way. First they must speak with me and remind me of their great service to me or my father. Perhaps their connection is through a bloodline or marriage. Once I have acknowledged their place, they retreat. Later, at camp, they will bring their wives and children and introductions will be made."

He glanced at her and smiled. "I do not flatter myself that so many people are interested in traveling with me. I have gone into the desert dozens of times. It is their future queen who sparks their imagination."

Daphne felt both flattered and guilty. She was happy to meet anyone interested in meeting her, but she hated the thought of letting them think her position as Murat's wife was permanent.

"Your eyes betray you," he said. "How tender your feelings for those you have not yet met. Perhaps if you opened your heart to your husband, you would be less troubled."

"Perhaps if my husband had bothered to win my affection instead of forcing something I never wanted, I could open my heart to him."

Instead of looking subdued or chagrined or even slightly guilty, Murat appeared pleased. "You have not called me that before."

"What?"

"Your husband."

How like him to only hear that part of the sentence. "Don't get too excited. I didn't mean it in a good way."

"Nevertheless it is true. We are bound." His gaze dropped to her midsection. "Perhaps by a child growing even now."

"Don't count on it."

She knew that if he had his way, he would will her to be pregnant. And if she had hers…she would be gone by morning.

Daphne breathed in the sweet air of the desert. The sounds delighted her—the laughter of the children, the jingling of the harnesses on the horses and camels, the call of the birds following them overhead.

As always the vastness of the wilderness left her feeling both small and yet very much a part of the world. All right—if truth be told, she would not wish herself away just yet. Perhaps it would be better if she left Murat *after* this trip.

"It has been many years since my people have had a queen to call their own," he said.

"Then you should encourage your father to remarry."

"He has had four wives and several great loves. I think he prefers his various mistresses."

"What man wouldn't?"

Murat's expression hardened. "Is that what you think? Do you resist me because you assume I will not keep my vows? I assure you, I have no interest in being with another woman. You are my wife and I seek solace in your bed alone."

Had things been different, the information would have thrilled her. As it was, she felt a slight flicker in her chest, but she quickly doused it.

"For now," she said.

"For always."

He drew his horse so close, her leg brushed against his.

"I am Crown Prince Murat of Bahania. My word is law. I will honor our vows to my death."

The declaration had the desired effect. She felt bad for doubting him and for the briefest moment wondered if she was being incredibly dumb to resist him. Yes, he'd married her against her will, but it wasn't as if he planned to mistreat her.

Wait! Was that her standard for a happy marriage? Lack of mistreatment? What about love and respect? What about treating each other with dignity? What about the fact that for the rest of their lives together, he would think it was all right to ignore her opinion and desires and simply do what he wanted?

"I plan to release you well before you breathe your last," she said.

His gaze narrowed. "You mock my sincerity."

"You ignore my deepest and most sincere wishes."

"I have not tried to bribe you."

She couldn't help laughing. "And that's a good thing?"

"I knew you would not approve. Nor would jewels and money influence your decision."

"You're right about that." How could he know her so well on the one hand and be such a jerk on the other? "You're very complicated."

He smiled. "Thank you."

"I'm not sure it's a compliment."

"Of course it is. You will not be bored with me."

That was true. "We'd fight a lot."

"Passion is healthy."

"Too much anger can chip away at the foundation of a relationship."

"I would not allow that to happen."

"You don't always get to choose."

"Of course I do. I am—"

She cut him off with a wave of her hand. "Yeah, yeah. Crown prince. Blah, blah, blah. You need some new material."

He stared at her with the shocked expression of a man hearing words from the mouth of a beetle. Both dark eyebrows raised, his mouth parted and she half expected him to stick his finger in his ear and jiggle it around.

"You dare to speak to me that way?"

"What's the problem. I am, for the moment at least, your wife. If I don't, who will?"

"No one. It is not permitted."

"Murat, you seem to be a pretty decent ruler, but you really have to get over yourself."

She half expected him to call down thunder onto her. Instead he stared at her for a long moment, then tossed his head back and began to laugh.

The sound delighted her, even as she realized she'd never heard it before. Oh, he'd laughed, but not like this—unrestrained, uncontrolled. He was not a man who allowed himself to be taken off guard very often.

In that moment she knew she could make a difference for him. She could be the person he trusted above all others, the person he depended upon. She could ease his burden, give him a safe place to rest.

Need filled her. All her life she had longed to be a part of something. She'd always felt out of step with her family, and since leaving home, she'd never found anyone to love that completely. With Murat...

He was a man who took what he wanted. She thought of all the dates she'd had with guys who didn't bother to call when they said they would or who were too intimidated by her family to want a relationship with her. Men who hadn't been strong.

Murat was too strong. They had been too weak. Was there any comfortable place in the middle? And if she had to choose one or the other, which was best?

Strength, she decided. Perhaps there was something to be said for a prince of the desert.

"What do you think?" Murat asked as he passed her a bowl filled with a spicy grain dish.

Daphne smiled. "It's amazing. I feel as if I'm in the middle of a giant movie."

A sea of tents surrounded them. Twilight approached, and in the growing dark, campfires stretched out toward the horizon. The last rays of the sun danced off the dozens of banners flying from tall poles.

Scents of a thousand meals prepared on open flames blended with perfumes and oils and the clean smell of fresh straw.

She and Murat dined alone. The guards were always there, ever-present shadows who watched for danger. Yet she felt comfortable and at peace. Should the unlikely occur and someone try to attack Murat, the intruder would be laid low long before he reached the center of the camp. The desert tribes were both fierce and loyal.

"While silence is often welcome in a woman," he said, "in your case it troubles me. What are you plotting?"

"I'm thinking about your people. They have a long and proud history."

"It is true. Many have sought to invade our land and none have succeeded. Now we have an air force to protect us from the skies." He picked up his glass of wine. "Why do I know you care more for the fate of my people than you care for me?"

"Because it's true," she said cheerfully before biting into a piece of chicken.

"You think you can say anything to me."

"Pretty much." She reached for her napkin. "What are you going to do to me? I'm the future queen. You can't really lock me up."

"There are other forms of punishment."

He spoke the words in a low voice that grated against her skin like burned velvet.

"Cheap threats," she told him. "I am the future queen. You must honor me."

"I already do."

"Not enough to admit you were sincerely wrong to hold me prisoner and marry me against my will."

"Perhaps we could put that behind us and move forward."

She glanced up toward the stars. "Oh, look. There's a flying camel."

He growled. "You mock me."

"I'm telling you what it will take for me to forgive and forget. It won't happen without you accepting your part in what you did."

"We will speak of something else."

"I had a feeling you'd say that." She reached for another piece of chicken.

The night was cool but pleasant. Murat sat across from her, looking completely at home in the primitive surroundings.

"Did you come out here much when you were younger?" she asked.

"When I could. There were many things for me to do back at the palace. Studies, lessons. I was presented to visiting dignitaries and expected to sit through many meetings. But when time permitted I escaped to the desert."

Where he could just be a boy. She could imagine him

riding hard and fast as he played with the other children. For an hour or two he wouldn't be the prince, and how he must have treasured that time.

Daphne shifted on her cushion. She wasn't used to sitting so low on the ground. As she got more comfortable, she noticed a group of people walking toward them. There were maybe seven or eight, both men and women. They took a few steps, stopped, seemed to argue among themselves, then moved forward again.

One of the guards rose and spoke with them. After a few minutes, they were waved forward. The walking, stopping, arguing continued as they got closer.

"I wonder what that's about?" she asked, nodding at them.

Murat followed her gaze. "They are not sure if they should interrupt us," he said. "The men resist, but the women insist. Some men should control their wives better."

"Some men are sensible enough to listen to a more intelligent opinion. What should we do?"

"Greet them."

Murat wiped his hands, then rose and helped her to her feet. They stood by the fire and waited as the small group approached.

Everyone bowed. One of the women elbowed one of the men but he didn't speak. Finally the woman took a step forward and bowed again.

"Greetings, Your Highness," she said, speaking to Daphne. "May the new day find you strong and healthy and blessed with good fortune always."

"May the new day find you equally blessed," Daphne replied.

"I fear it will not."

"We should not be here," one of the men said. He looked at Murat. "We are sorry to have troubled you and your bride."

"No!" The woman glared at him. "We are in need."

"How can we help?" Daphne asked.

The woman sighed. "A family who travels with us has a camel in labor. There is trouble of some kind. The man who usually helps with such things did not come with us. We have heard that you are trained with animals. Is it true?"

Daphne took in their robes. While the cloth was clean, it had been mended and patched in several places. She doubted these people could afford to lose a healthy, breeding camel.

The man with her grabbed her arm. "In all this crowd, there must be one other who can assist us. You should not bother the wife of the crown prince."

"There is no time," the woman said. "The mother grows weak." She looked at Daphne. "Please help us."

Daphne wasn't sure of the protocol of the situation. Nor did she know if she could help. "I've never delivered a camel before," she admitted. "I've had a lot of experience with cows and horses. If that is good enough."

The woman sagged with relief. "Yes. Please. A thousand thanks. This way." Then she hurried off.

Daphne started to follow her and wasn't all that surprised when Murat and his guards fell into step.

"You have delivered cows and horses?" he asked. "In Chicago?"

"No. In the country. It's not all that far to the farmlands in the south. I would spend a few months there every summer. Nothing against your father and his hundred or so cats, but it was always a nice change to work on big animals instead of small house pets."

As she walked, she shrugged out of her robes, handing them to Murat who passed them on to a guard. By the time they reached the straw-lined enclosure, she was down to her jeans and a T-shirt. Both of which were going to be pretty yucky by the time this was done. Birth was never tidy.

Three hours later a baby camel teetered on spindly legs. His mother moved close and nudged him until he began to nurse. Daphne leaned against the makeshift fence and smiled. This was the part she liked best—after, when things had gone well.

"Impressive," Murat said, stepping out of the shadows and moving close. "You were very confident."

"All that medical training paid off." She stretched. "I didn't think you'd stick around. It's late."

"I wanted to see what happened." He put an arm around her and led her away from the pen. "While you were working, I spoke with some of the elders of the tribe. The mother has died and the father is ill. There are three boys who tend the family's small herd. They desperately needed this birth."

"I'm glad I didn't know that," she admitted. "I wouldn't have liked the pressure."

"Had the camel died, I would have compensated them, but you were able to give them back their livelihood."

There was pride in his voice, which surprised her. Her parents had never thought much of what she did for a living, why should Murat?

He pulled her close, but she resisted. "I'm pretty stinky," she said. "I don't suppose we have a shower in our tent."

"No, but I can provide you with a bath."

"Really?"

"Of course."

Their massive private tent had still been under construction at dinner so she hadn't had a chance to see the interior. Now she followed Murat inside to a foyerlike opening. They removed their shoes. He held open a flap, and she stepped into an amazing world she hadn't known existed.

The fabric ceiling stretched up at least ten feet. Carpets were piled on top of each other underfoot. Her toes curled into the exquisite patterns and softness.

Low benches and plush chairs provided seating around carved tables. Old-fashioned lamps hung from hooks, providing illumination. The faint but steady rumble of a generator explained the flow of fresh, cool air she felt on her face.

"This way," he said and led her deeper into the tent.

There was a dining area, a huge bed on a dais, and a tub filled with steaming water that nearly made her moan with delight.

She had to resist the urge to dive in headfirst. Instead she tugged off her socks, then glanced down at her filthy T-shirt.

"Good thing I didn't pack light," she said. "I think this one is past recovering."

Murat shrugged out of his robes and left them draped over a low chair. Then, wearing only loose trousers and a white shirt, he moved close and held out his hand.

"What?" she asked.

"Your clothing."

She took a step back. "I'm not getting undressed in front of you."

"You forget. I have seen you bare before."

"That's not the point."

Actually, it was exactly the point. Getting naked with Murat around would only lead to trouble. Even talking about it made her body start to react. Tiny pinpricks of desire nipped at her skin. Her belly felt hollow and hot and an ache took up residence between her thighs.

"I'm perfectly capable of bathing myself," she said.

"I am offering to help." His dark gaze caught her and wouldn't let her go.

"Not necessary."

"Are you afraid?"

"Murat, I'm not playing that game. Now shoo so I can get cleaned up."

Instead of leaving, he moved closer. "I am here to help you with your bath, my most stubborn princess. I give you my word that I will make no attempt to seduce you in your bath. I will not make suggestive remarks or touch you in any inappropriate way. Now, take off your clothes."

Was this how the cobra felt in the face of the snake charmer, she wondered. She didn't want to listen or do as he said, yet she found herself reaching for the hem of her T-shirt and pulling the whole thing off, over her head. She handed it to Murat.

Her jeans were next, leaving her in a bra and panties. Turning her back on him, she unfastened the former and pushed down the latter. They tumbled to the carpeted ground. Then she stepped into the steaming tub and sank down into the water.

The heat soothed aching muscles. She reached up to keep her hair out of the water, but Murat had moved behind the tub and brushed her hands away.

"I will do it," he said as he gently coiled her hair, then took pins from a nearby tray and secured her hair on top of her head.

"Here."

He handed her a bar of scented soap and a washcloth. She breathed in the smell of flowers and sandalwood.

The water was clear, which made her feel awkward about being naked. Murat stayed behind her, and there weren't any mirrors, so she tried to tell herself he wasn't really there…watching. Still, as she smoothed the soapy washcloth across her suddenly sensitive breasts, she felt his gaze on her.

She turned only to find him with his back to the tub.

He stood by the wooden dresser, opening a drawer and drawing out a nightgown. Okay, so her imagination was putting in some overtime. Obviously he'd meant what he said. This was just a bath.

Being female and completely comfortable supporting two opposite ideas at exactly the same time, her next thought was one of annoyance. Didn't he *notice* that she was naked? Didn't he find her sexually appealing? Wasn't he aroused by the situation? They were married, and a man was supposed to want his wife.

She quickly finished washing and wrung out the cloth. Annoyance made her slosh the water as she stood. "Could you hand me a towel?" she asked.

Murat reached for one and handed it to her. From what she could tell, he barely looked at her naked, wet body. How perfect. Now that he had her, he didn't want her anymore. Just like a man, she thought as she rubbed herself dry. Fine. She could "not want" him, too.

She wrapped the towel around herself and stepped out of the tub. He passed her a nightgown. The soft, pale silk was unfamiliar, but at this point she was too much in a temper to care. She let the towel drop to the floor and slid the nightgown over her head.

The see-through fabric left nothing to the imagination. The front dipped down nearly to her stomach, and the back consisted of a few lacy straps and nothing else. Ha! As if Murat would care.

She wanted to kick him. She walked to stalk out into the night and scream her frustration to the heavens. What was wrong with him not to react? And more important, why did she care? She didn't love Murat. Lately she didn't even like him very much. So why did it bother her that he hadn't pounced on her like a cat on catnip?

"I'm going to bed," she said curtly. "Good night."

"You enjoyed your bath?" he asked from his place just behind her.

"It was fine."

"You would consider it finished now?"

She turned until she could look at him. "As I'm out of it, dry and dressed, I would go with yes."

"Good."

A rush of movement followed the word and she found herself caught up against him as he hauled her into his arms and pressed his mouth to hers.

She had no time to think or react or even feel. His hands were everywhere. Her back, her sides, her breasts. He kissed her hotly, ravishing her. Somehow she managed to part her lips, and he swept inside with the purposefulness of a man set on claiming his woman.

Even as he cupped her breast and stroked her hard nipple through the thin fabric of her nightgown, he squeezed her rear and pulled her into him. She felt the pulsing hardness of his arousal.

"You want me," she murmured, her mouth still against his.

He raised his head and stared at her. "Of course. Why would you think otherwise?"

"Because I was naked and you just ignored me."

"I gave you my word I would not bother you while you were in your bath."

Of all the times for him to keep it, this would not have been her first choice.

"You're the most annoying man," she told him.

He bent down and swept her into his arms. "Let me annoy you some more," he said as he carried her to the bed on the other side of the tent.

There were candles hanging everywhere and fresh-cut flowers in vases all over the room. The white linens had been folded back invitingly. Murat knelt on the mattress, then lowered her onto the smooth surface.

She kept her arms around his neck and pulled him close so she could kiss him.

Once again he claimed her with a kiss that marked her as his. She supposed she should protest, or at least not like it so much, but she couldn't help squirming in delight as he nipped on her lower lip, then drew the sensitive curve into his mouth. He nibbled her jaw and down her throat. Lower and lower until he settled over her tight, aching nipples.

The silk was so thin, he didn't bother pushing it away. Instead he licked and sucked her through the fabric. She ran her fingers through his hair, to touch him as much as to hold him in place. He moved to her other breast, repeating the glorious touching and teasing, until she felt hot and strung far too tightly.

Wanting poured through her. She couldn't seem to keep her legs still, and between her thighs a pulsing hunger began.

"Murat," she breathed as she began to tug at his shirt. "I need you."

"No more than I need you." He took the hint and shrugged out of the garment.

She took advantage of his distraction to pull up her nightgown in a shameless invitation. She knew this wasn't her smartest act of the day, but she couldn't seem to stem the tide of need rushing through her. She might have had other lovers, but she'd never wanted one the way she wanted Murat. Desperation made her reach for his trousers. He had to be in her. Now!

"Impatient?" he asked with a smile as he shed the rest of his clothing, then slipped between her legs. "Let me take the edge off, my sweet."

Instead of filling her with his hardness, he bent low and gently parted her swollen flesh with his fingers. Then he pressed his mouth against her hot, damp center.

She had only a second to brace herself before the impact of the pleasure nearly had her screaming down the tent. Vaguely mindful of their neighbors, she held in her cries of delight as he licked all of her before settling on that one single point of pleasure.

He traced quick circles, making her breathe more quickly. Tension made her dig in her heels and grab on to the covers. She tossed her head from side to side as he gently sucked that one perfect spot.

She rocked her hips in time with his movements, moving closer and closer to her ultimate release. Every brush of his tongue, every whisper of breath pushed her onward. When she finally clung to the edge, so ready to surrender all to him, he slipped two fingers inside of her.

The combination was too much. She tried to hold

back, to enjoy the moment longer, but it wasn't possible. Passion claimed her and she called out Murat's name as she sank into the waves of pleasure.

Fast, at first, then slowing, but not really ever ending. Not even when he raised his head and stared at her with wild, hungry eyes. He continued to move his fingers. Back and forth, back and forth. Mini-waves rippled through her. Climax after climax. As long as he touched her, she came.

She stared at him, unable to control her body's response to his touch.

"Murat," she breathed.

He shifted closer, at last replacing his fingers with his arousal. He thrust into her, filling her until she thought she might shatter.

It was too good. There was too much. She came again and again. Every time he moved into her, she gave herself over to the release. Faster and faster until they were both breathing hard, and then she lost herself again in a violent shuddering that left her both shattered and satisfied down to her bones.

Chapter Twelve

Daphne awoke the next morning with the sense of being one with the world. She could hear the birds outside and the low voices of people in the encampment. The smell of cooking made her mouth water, and the sounds of laughter made her smile. She had a feeling that when she climbed out of bed, there was a very good chance she would float several inches above the carpeted tent floor.

What a night, she thought as she pushed her hair out of her face and sat up. Murat was long gone. She vaguely recalled him kissing her before he'd left their bed sometime after dawn.

They'd continued to make love, each time more passionately than the time before until she'd been afraid she would never be able to recover. Her body ached, but in the best way possible. Her skin seemed to be glowing, and she knew she would be hard-pressed not to spend the entire day grinning like a fool.

Everything had been perfect. Except… She pressed her hands to her flat stomach and wondered if they'd made a baby last night. She and Murat had made love several times without any kind of protection. The thought had never crossed her mind. She knew the price of having his child—she would never be able to leave.

Now, in the soft light of the morning in the beautiful tent, she wondered if perhaps she should make her peace with all that had happened. Was his behavior really that horrible? He'd only—

"Earth to Daphne," she said aloud. "Let's think about this."

Rational thought returned, pushing away the lingering effects of the night of pleasure. Of course she couldn't give in. Even if she wanted to stay married to Murat, she would still need to make him understand that he couldn't have his way in everything. That for their marriage to be a happy and successful union, they both had to make decisions, and he couldn't simply bully his way into what he wanted.

Which meant getting pregnant was a really dumb idea. She was going to have to avoid his bed.

She stood and faced the rumpled sheets. It was a very nice bed and the man who slept in it was nothing short of magical when it came to making love. Still, she had to be strong. At least until she knew if she were pregnant.

She washed using the basin of water on the dresser, then pulled on the garments that had been left out for her. Murat had mentioned something about a tribal council today. He would assemble the leaders from the various tribes and then hear judgments and petitions from the people. She'd agreed to attend.

Intricate embroidery covered her robes. In place of a headdress, a small diamond-and-gold crown sat on a pillow.

Daphne stared at it. While she knew that Murat was the crown prince and that he would one day be king, she never really thought about it all that seriously. But now, staring at the crown, she felt the weight of a thousand years of history pressing on her.

She carefully brushed her long, blond hair until it gleamed, then she set the crown on her head and secured it with two pins. She checked that it was straight, all the while trying not to notice she actually had it on her head, then left for the main part of the tent.

One of Murat's security agents sat waiting for her. When she approached, he stood and bowed.

"Good morning, Princess Daphne," he said. "The judgments are about to begin. If you will follow me."

He led her outside into a beautiful, clear morning. The camp was nearly deserted, but up ahead she saw a huge covering that would easily hold a thousand people. They walked toward it, avoiding the main entrance and instead circling around to the back.

She ducked under a low hanging and found herself behind a dais that held several ornate chairs. Murat approached and took her hand in his.

"We are about to begin," he said with a smile.

He spoke easily, but his eyes sent her another message. One that reminded her of their night together and all that had happened between them.

She wanted to tell him they couldn't do that again. Not until things were straightened out between them, but this was not the time or place.

She followed him up onto the dais and sat in a chair just to the left and slightly behind his. On his right sat the tribal council. In front of them were hundreds of people sitting in rows. A few stood on either side of the room, and an older man with a parchment scroll stood in the center.

He read from the ancient document in a language she didn't recognize. She remembered enough from her previous time in Bahania to know he called all those seeking justice to this place and time. That the prince's word would be final. Judgments against those charged with crimes were covered in the morning, while petitions came in the afternoon.

Several criminals were brought forward. Two charges were dismissed as being brought about by a desire for revenge rather than an actual crime. One man accused of stealing goats was sentenced to six months in a prison and a branding.

Daphne winced at the latter and Murat caught the movement.

"It is an old way," he said, turning toward her. "A man is given three chances. The brand allows the council to know how many times he has been before them."

"But branding?"

"He stole," Murat said. "These are desert people. They exist hundreds and thousands of miles from the world as you know it. If you steal a man's car in the city, he can walk or take a bus. You steal a man's goats or camels in the desert and you sentence him and his family to possible death. They may starve before they can walk out of the desert or to another encampment. They would not be able to carry all their possessions themselves, so they would be discarded. The youngest children might die on the long walk to safety. Stealing is not something we take lightly."

His words made sense. Daphne understood that where life was harsh, punishment must be equally so, but the whole concept made her uncomfortable.

Several more minor cases were brought forward. Then a man in his late twenties was walked in front of the dais.

The guards took his left arm and held it out for all to see. Three brands scarred his skin. Daphne sucked in a breath.

"He is charged with stealing camels," a member of the council told Murat.

"Witnesses?"

Five people stepped behind the men. Two were his accomplices, while the other three—a father and two sons—had owned the camels. The father spoke about the night his camels were taken. He had a herd of twenty, and this man and his friends took all of them. He and his sons went after the thieves only to find that one of the camels had gone lame and the thieves had slit its throat.

The crowd gasped. Daphne knew that to kill such a useful creature because it had gone lame was considered an abomination.

The cohorts spoke of the crime. They had already been charged and had confessed. Each had a fresh brand—their only brand. But the leader had three.

Murat listened to all the evidence, then turned to the council.

"Death," each of them said.

When it was his turn to speak, he said, "You decided not to end your thieving yourself. We will do it for you."

The criminal dropped his head to his chest. "I have two children and no wife."

Murat nodded for the children to be brought out.

A boy of maybe fourteen stepped forward, holding on to the hand of a much younger girl. The boy fought tears, but the little girl seemed more confused, as if she didn't understand what was happening.

"What of this?" Murat asked the boy. "Do you have a brand on your arm?"

The teenager squared his shoulders. "I do not steal, Prince Murat. I protect my sister and honor the memory of my mother."

"Very well." Murat turned his attention to the crowd. "Two children of the thief."

There was a moment of silence, then a tall man in his early forties stepped toward the dais.

"I will take them," he said.

Murat was silent.

The man nodded. "I give my word that they will be treated well and raised as my own. The boy will be given the opportunity to attend college if he likes."

Daphne glared at the man and raised her eyebrows.

He caught her gaze and took a step back. "Ah, the girl, too."

"Better," she murmured.

"She-wolf," Murat whispered back. But he sounded pleased.

Still Murat did not speak to the man making the offer. At last the man sighed. He called out to the crowd. Several people turned to watch as a young girl of eleven or so stepped out and walked to the man.

"My youngest," he said heavily. "The daughter of my heart. I give her into your keeping, to ensure the safety of those I take in."

The girl stared up at him. "Papa?"

He patted her head. "All will be well, child."

Murat rose. "I agree," he said. "The children of the thief will enter a new family. Their pasts will be washed clean and they will not carry their father's burden."

He walked to Daphne and held out his hand. She stood and took it, then followed him off the dais, toward the rear of the tent.

"What was all that?" she asked. "Why did that man bring out his daughter?"

"Because she is insurance. We will check on the condition of the two children he is taking in, but here, desert traditions run deep. Should he not treat them well, they will be removed from his care, along with his daughter. She gives him incentive to keep his word."

She'd never heard of such a thing. "An interesting form of foster care."

"It is more than that. He will take those children into his home and treat them as his own. I meant what I said—they will not bear the stigma of their father's crimes." He urged her toward their tent. "It is often this way with the children of criminals. They are taken in and given a good home. I have never heard of one of them being ill treated. I know the man who claimed them. He will be good to them."

She ducked into the tent and found lunch waiting for them. "I guess it really does take a village."

"For us it does."

He held out her chair, then took the seat across from hers. A young woman carried a tray of food toward them.

"What happens this afternoon?" Daphne asked as she served herself some salad. "More criminals?"

"No. The petitions. Anyone may approach me directly and ask me to settle a dispute."

"That must keep you busy."

He smiled. "Not as busy as you would think. My word is law, and I have a reputation of being stern and difficult. Only the truly brave seek my form of justice."

"Are you fair?" she asked.

He shrugged. "The fate of my people rests in my

hands. I do not take that responsibility lightly. I do my best to see both sides of the situation and find the best solution for all concerned."

He wasn't what she thought. At first she'd described Murat as being just like her family—friendly and supportive as long as he got his way. But now she questioned that. He wanted to be a good leader. A good man.

How did she reconcile that with what he'd done to her? What was the solution to her dilemma? How did she show him that they had to be honest with each other before they had any hope of a relationship together?

After lunch Murat met with his tribal council, and Daphne went for a walk. She strolled by the makeshift stables and stopped to watch several children play soccer. A young woman approached and bowed.

"Greetings, Princess," she said. "I am Aisha. It is a great honor to meet you."

"The honor is mine," Daphne said with a smile.

The girl was maybe sixteen or seventeen and incredibly beautiful. In the safety of the camp, she left her head uncovered. Her large brown eyes crinkled slightly at the corners as if she found life amusing. Her full mouth curved up at the corners. Jewelry glinted from her ears and caught the sunlight.

"I must confess I sought you out on purpose," Aisha said. "I have a petition for the prince, but I dare not deliver it myself."

"Why?"

The girl ducked her head. "My father has forbidden me."

Daphne didn't like the sound of that. "He forbids you to seek justice?"

She shrugged. "He has offered me in marriage to a man in our tribe. The man is very honorable and wealthy. Instead of my father having to provide me with a dowry, the man will pay *him* the price of five camels."

This would be the part of the old-fashioned desert world Daphne didn't like so much. "Is your potential fiancé much older?"

Aisha nodded. "He is nearly fifty and has many children older than me. He swears he loves me and I am to be his last wife, but…"

"You don't love him."

"I…" The girl swallowed. "I have given my heart to another," she said in a whisper. "I know it's wrong," she added in a rush. "I have defied my father and dishonored my family. I know I should be punished. But marriage to someone so old seems harsh. Please, Princess Daphne, as the wife of the crown prince you are entitled to plead on my behalf. The prince will listen to you."

Daphne thought about her own recent marriage and the circumstances involved. "I'm not the right person to take this to the prince. You have to believe me."

"You are my only hope." Tears filled Aisha's eyes. "I beg you."

The girl reached for the gold bangles on her wrists. "Take my jewelry. Take everything I have."

"No." Daphne shook her head. "You don't need to pay for my support. I…"

Now what? She felt bad for the girl, but would Murat give his new wife a fair hearing in these circumstances? He had said he took his responsibility very seriously. She would have to trust that…and him.

"I'll do it," she said. "Tell me what you want from the prince."

Murat listened as the woman explained why she was entitled to have her dowry returned to her. Her case was strong and in the end, he agreed. The husband, who had only married her for her dowry, sputtered and complained, but Murat stared him down and he retreated. Murat spoke with the leaders of the woman's tribe to make sure there would be no retribution and gave her permission to contact his office directly if his wishes weren't followed out.

Next two men argued over the use of a small spring deep in the desert. Murat gave his ruling, then watched as a veiled woman approached. By the time she'd taken a second step, he knew it was Daphne.

Why did she seek him so publicly? To petition for her own freedom?

For a moment he considered the possibility. That she would seek to hold him to the fairness he claimed to offer all. A protest rose within him. There were no words, just the sense that she couldn't leave. Then he remembered their night of lovemaking and the one that had occurred nearly three weeks before. She could not go until they were sure she was not with child. More than anyone, she understood the law of the land.

Relief quickly followed, allowing him to relax as she walked toward him. As she reached the dais, she bowed low, then flipped back her head covering to reveal her features. Many in the waiting crowd gasped.

"I seek justice at the hand of Crown Prince Murat," she said, then frowned slightly. "You're not surprised it's me."

"I recognized your walk."

"I was covered."

"A husband knows such things."

Several of the women watching smiled.

He leaned forward. "Why do you seek my justice? For yourself?"

"No. For another. I call forward Aisha."

A young woman no more than sixteen or seventeen moved next to Daphne. Murat held in a groan. He had a bad feeling he knew what had happened. The girl had approached Daphne and had told a sad story about being forced to marry someone she didn't love. Daphne had agreed to petition on her behalf.

Murat looked at the teenager. "Why do you not petition for yourself?" he asked.

The girl, a beauty, with honey-colored skin and hair that hung to her waist, dropped her chin and stared at the ground. "My father forbade me to do so."

Murat shifted back in his chair and waited. Sure enough, someone started pushing through the waiting throng. A man stepped forward and bowed low.

"Prince Murat, a thousand blessings on you and your family."

Murat didn't speak.

The man twisted his hands together, bowed again, then cleared his throat. "She is but a child. A foolish young girl who dreams of the stars."

Murat didn't doubt that, but the law was the law. "Everyone is entitled to petition the prince. Even a foolish young girl."

"Yes. Of course you are correct. I never dreamed she would seek out your most perfect and radiant wife. May you have a hundred sons. May they be long-lived and fruitful. May—"

Murat raised his hand to cut off the frantic praise. No doubt the thought of a hundred sons had sent Daphne into a panic. He looked at her and raised his eyebrows.

"You see what you have started?"

"I seek only what is right."

Murat sighed and turned his attention to the girl. "All right. Aisha. You have the attention of the prince, and your father is not going to stop you from stating your case. What do you want from me?"

It was as he expected. Her father wished her to marry an old man with many children.

"I am the wife he expects to care for him in his waning years," she said in outrage.

"And the man in question?" Murat asked.

There was more movement in the crowd, and a tall, bearded man stepped forward. He had to be in his late fifties. He bore himself well and had the appearance of prosperity about him.

The man bowed. "I am Farid," he said in a low voice.

"You wish to marry this girl?" Murat asked.

Farid nodded. "She is a good girl and will serve me well."

"Instead of asking for a dowry, he offers me five camels," the father said eagerly. "He has been married before and has lost each wife to illness. Very sad. But all in the village agree the women were well treated."

Murat felt the beginnings of a headache coming on. He looked at the girl.

"There is one more player missing, is there not?"

Aisha nodded slowly. "Barak. The man I love."

Her father gasped in outrage, the fiancé looked patiently indulgent and a steady rumble rose from the crowd.

At last Barak appeared. He was all of twenty-two or twenty-three. Defiant and terrified at the same time. He bowed low before Murat.

"You love Aisha, as well?" Murat asked.

The young man glanced at her, then nodded. "With all my heart. I have been saving money, buying camels. With her dowry, we can buy three more and have a good-size herd. I can provide for her."

"I will not give her a dowry," her father said. "Not for you. Farid is a good man. A better match."

"Especially for you," Murat said. "To be given camels for your daughter instead of having to pay them makes it a fine match."

The father did not speak.

Murat studied Farid. There was something about the color of the skin around his eyes. A grayness.

"You have sons?" Murat asked the older man.

"Six, Your Highness."

"All married?"

"Two are not."

Murat saw the picture more clearly now. "How long do you have?" he asked Farid.

The man looked surprised by the question, but he recovered quickly. "At most a year."

"What?" the girl's father asked. "What are you talking about?"

Murat shook his head. "It is of no matter." He rose and nodded at his wife. "If you will come with me."

He led her to the rear of the tent.

"What's going on?" Daphne wanted to know. "Can you do this? Stop the hearing or whatever it is in midsentence? What about Aisha? Are you going to force her to marry that horrible old man?"

Murat touched her long, blond hair. "That horrible old man is dying. He has less than a year to live."

"Oh. Well, I'm sorry to hear that, but the information means Aisha was right. He's buying her to take care of him in his old age. If he's so rich, why doesn't he just hire a nurse?"

"Because this isn't about his health. It's about his wealth. Farid has six sons. Two are not married. Per our laws, he must leave everything to them equally, which divides his fortune into small pieces. But that is not the best way to maintain wealth in the family. What if the sons do not get along? What if their wives want them to take the inheritance to their own families? If Farid dies married, he can leave forty percent of what he has to his wife. The rest is split among his children. I believe his plan is for one of his unmarried sons to then marry Aisha and together they will run the family business."

Daphne looked outraged. "Great. So she's to be sold, not once but twice? That's pleasant."

"You are missing the point. Farid doesn't want her for himself."

"I get the point exactly. Either way she's been given in marriage to someone she doesn't know or care about. And she's in love with someone else. What about that?"

Why did Daphne refuse to see the sense of the union? "She could be a wealthy widow in her own right in just a few months," he said. "She wouldn't have to marry one of the sons if she didn't want to."

"Are you saying she should agree to this? That in a few months, she could bring in what's his name—"

"Barak."

"Right. She could bring in Barak? That's terrible, too."

Murat shook his head. "Marriage isn't just about love, Daphne. It is about political and financial gain."

"I see that now. What are you going to do?"

"What do you want me to do?"

She raised her eyebrows. "It's my choice?"

"Yes. Consider it a wedding gift."

"I want Aisha to have the choice to follow her heart. I want her to be free to marry Barak."

"Despite what I have told you?"

She stared at him. "Not despite it, but *because* of it."

"And years from now, when she and Barak are struggling to feed their many children, do you not think she will look back on what she could have had and feel regret?"

"Not if she loves him."

"Love does not put food on the table." Love was not practical. Why did women consider it so very important?

"I want her to be with Barak," Daphne insisted.

"As you wish."

He led her back to the dais and took his seat. Aisha had been crying, and her father looked furious. Farid seemed resigned, while the young lover, Barak, attempted to appear confident even as his shaking knees gave him away.

Murat looked at Aisha. "You chose your petitioner well. Daphne is my bride and, as such, I can refuse her nothing. I grant your request, but listen to me well. You are angry that your father would sell you to a man so many years older. You see only today and tomorrow. There is all of your future to consider. Farid is a man of great honor. Will you not consider him?"

Aisha shook her head. "I love Barak," she said stubbornly.

Murat glanced at the boy and hoped he would be worthy of her devotion. "Very well. Aisha is free to marry Barak."

Her father started to sputter, but Murat quelled him with a quick glare.

"I give them three camels in celebration of their marriage. May their union be long and healthy."

Aisha began to cry. Barak bowed low several times, then gathered his fiancée in his arms and whispered to her.

Murat turned to the angry father. "I give you three camels, as well, in compensation for what you have lost in your deal with Farid."

Murat knew that Farid had offered five camels, but he wasn't about to give the father more than he gave the couple.

Finally he looked at Farid. "When it is your time, your family may bring you to the mountain of the kings."

The crowd gasped. The honor of being buried in such a place was unheard of.

Farid bowed low. "I give thanks to the good and wise prince. I wish that I would live to see you rule as king."

"I wish that, as well. Go in peace, my friend." Murat then waited as they all left.

"Who is next?" he asked.

Daphne stayed quiet during dinner. Murat seemed tense and restless. He had been that way since returning to their tent.

When the last plate had been cleared away, she put down her napkin and smiled. "I want to thank you again for what you did today."

"I do not wish to speak of it."

"Why not? You made Aisha very happy."

"I granted the wish of a spoiled girl. She is too young to know her heart. Do you really believe she will love that boy for very long? And then what? She will be poor and hate her husband. At least her father sought to secure her future."

Daphne couldn't believe Murat actually thought the marriage of a sixteen-year-old to a man four times her age was a good thing.

"Her father wanted to sell her," she said in outrage. "That's pretty horrible."

"I agree, the father's motives were suspect, but Farid was a good man, and she would have had financial security."

"Right. To be sold again into marriage with one of his sons."

"She might have fallen in love with one as well."

"Or she might not."

Murat stared at her as if she were a complete idiot. "As a widow, she would be free to marry whomever she liked. No one could force her into the marriage."

"Gee, so it's only the one time. That makes it all right."

He turned away. "You do not understand our ways and our customs."

"I don't think it's that, at all. I think you're angry because I petitioned for the girl."

He stood and glared at her. "I am angry because my wife took the side of a foolish young woman and I did as she requested. I am angry because I believe Aisha chose poorly."

He stopped talking, but she sensed there was more. Something much larger than Aisha and her problems. But what?

Murat walked away from the table into the sitting area of the tent. She followed him.

"You gave a woman her freedom, Murat. What is so terrible about that?"

"What is so terrible about our marriage?" he asked. "Why do you seek to escape?"

Was that it? Did he see her in Aisha?

"I'm not in love with anyone else," she told him. "I would have told you if I was."

"I never considered the matter," he said, but she wasn't sure she believed him.

"Being married to you isn't terrible," she said slowly, still not sure what they were arguing about. "My objection is to the way it happened. You never asked."

"I did and you refused."

"Right. And you went ahead and married me, anyway. You can't do that."

"I can and I did."

She couldn't believe it. "You say that like it's a good thing."

"Achieving my goal is always a good thing." He moved toward her. "We are married now. You will accept that."

"I won't."

"And if you carry my child?"

Daphne pressed both hands to her stomach. They should know fairly quickly. "I'm not."

"You are not yet sure." He loomed over her. "Make no mistake. Any child will stay here. You may leave if you like."

"I would never leave my baby behind."

"Then the decision is made for you."

She wanted to scream. She wanted to demand that he understand. Why was he being so stubborn and hateful?

"I won't sleep with you again," she said.

"So you told me before, yet look what happened."

She felt as if he'd slapped her. "Is that all that night meant to you? Was it just a chance to prove me wrong?"

"Your word means very little."

She turned away, both because it hurt to look at him and to keep him from seeing the tears in her eyes.

"I'm sorry I came on this trip with you," she said. "I wish I'd never left the palace."

"If you prefer to be back there, it can be arranged."

"Then go ahead and do it."

Chapter Thirteen

Murat left the tent without looking back. Daphne wasn't sure what to do, so she stayed where she was. Less than forty minutes later she heard the sound of a helicopter approaching. One of the security agents came and got her, and before she could figure out what had happened, she found herself being whisked up into the night sky.

The glow of all the campfires seemed to stretch out for miles. She pressed her fingers against the cool glass window and wished for a second chance to take back the angry words she and Murat had exchanged.

He'd hurt her. She refused to believe he'd spent last night making love with her only to prove a point. Their time together had to have meant something to him, too. But why wouldn't he admit it? And why had he let her go so easily?

Just like before, she thought sadly, when she'd broken their engagement. He'd let her go without trying to stop her then, too.

The trip back to the palace took less than thirty minutes. She made her way to the suite she shared with Murat and let herself inside.

Everything was as she'd left it, except that the man she'd married was gone. She had no idea when he would return or what they would say to each other when he did.

She wandered through the room, touching pictures and small personal things, his pen or a pair of cuff links. She missed him. How crazy was that?

Something brushed against her leg. She looked down and saw one of the king's cats rubbing against her. She picked up the animal and held it close. The warm body and soft purr comforted her. Still holding the cat, she sank down on the sofa and began to cry.

"So, how was it?" Billie asked the next morning as she threw herself on one of the sofas. "I can't imagine riding through the desert. Flying would get you there much faster."

Cleo sat next to her sister-in-law and swatted her with a pillow. "The journey is the point. When you fly you never get to see anything."

"Yeah, but you get there fast." Billie grinned. "I'm into the whole speed thing."

"And we didn't know that." Cleo fluffed her short, blond hair. "Did you have a good time? I thought you would have been gone longer."

"It was great," Daphne said, hoping the cold compresses she'd used earlier had taken down some of the swelling around her eyes. Crying herself to sleep never made for a pretty morning after. "I enjoyed the riding, and the tent was incredible. Like something out of *Arabian Nights.* There were dozens of rugs underfoot, hanging lights and a really huge bathtub."

Billie smoothed the front of her skirt over her very pregnant belly. "Tubs can be fun. Anything you want to talk about?"

"Not really," Daphne said, trying to keep things light. "The cultural differences were interesting. I enjoyed watching Murat work with the council."

"You weren't gone long enough to get to the City of Thieves, were you?" Cleo asked, then covered her mouth. She winced and dropped her hand. "Tell me Murat told you about it. I *so* don't want to be shot at dawn."

"Not to worry. He did. And, no, I didn't make it there."

She'd been looking forward to it, too. She hadn't really wanted to leave the caravan. She'd acted impulsively in the moment. Why had she reacted so strongly last night? Why had he been so willing to fight with her and let her go?

"I wanted to see Sabrina and meet Zara," she said.

"They're both very cool," Cleo said. "You'll have time later. Or we could plan a lunch. The show-off here can fly us out there in a helicopter."

"Cleo's just jealous because I'm talented," Billie said with a grin.

"It's disgusting," Cleo admitted. "And she brags about it all the time."

"Do not."

"Do, too."

Daphne felt a wave of longing. These women weren't sisters, yet they were closer than Daphne had ever been to anyone in her family. If she stayed, she could be a part of this, as well.

If.

Cleo shifted to the edge of the sofa and laced her hands together. "I'm not sure how to say this delicately, so I'm just going to blurt it out. Something's up. You're obviously unhappy. You're back early and Murat isn't with you. Given how you two came to be married and all, Billie and I were wondering if you wanted to talk. You don't have to, but we're here to listen."

Daphne bit her lower lip. She did want to confide in someone, but… "You're both in very different places."

"Okay." Billie looked confused. "I know you mean more than us sitting on the sofa and you sitting on a chair."

Daphne couldn't help laughing. Cleo stared at Billie and rolled her eyes.

"She means we're in love with our husbands and she's not sure she is." She glanced at Daphne. "Is that right?"

"Yes."

"I knew that," Billie said. "I guess you have a point. But Murat isn't so bad, is he?"

"I don't know."

Daphne realized it was the truth. That while she hated what he'd done to her—how he'd used circumstances and manipulated her to get what he wanted—she wasn't sure how she felt about the man himself.

"There's the whole 'going to be queen thing,'" Cleo said. "Does that count for anything?"

"Of course it doesn't," Billie said. "Daphne has more depth than that."

Cleo sighed. "I actually wasn't asking you."

"Do you two ever stop arguing?"

"Sure," Cleo said. "When we're not together." She linked arms with her sister-in-law. "Billie and I have fabulous chemistry. I love sniping at her more than almost anything. It's like a sporting event."

Billie nodded. "Jefri and Sadik have gotten used to never getting a word in edgewise when the four of us have dinner."

"Shopping is a complete nightmare for the guys," Cleo said. "We have credit cards and we know how to use them." She disentangled her arm. "How can you not want to be a part of this?"

"You're tempting me."

"More than being queen?"

Daphne curled up in the chair and leaned her head against the back. "I remember when I was here before. I was so young, just twenty, and engaged to Murat. The thought of being queen really terrified me. I was sort of a serious kid, and I knew there would be huge responsibilities. I didn't think I could ever manage."

"And now?" Billie asked.

"I don't know. There's a part of me that thinks I could really help Murat. He doesn't have anyone he can confide in. Not to say anything against his brothers."

Cleo and Billie looked at each other, then at her. "I know what you mean," Cleo said. "Sadik is in meetings with Murat and that kind of thing, but he only has to worry about his own area of expertise. Murat has all the responsibility. King Hassan is handing over more and more of the day-to-day ruling. So a wife he trusted could help lighten the load."

"Maybe. I think I could make a difference. As much as I don't get along with my family, I have to admit I've been raised to be married to a powerful man."

"How nice not to have to learn what fork goes where," Billie grumbled.

Daphne grinned. "It's a skill that has served me well."

"So you're okay with the office of queen, which means the problem lies with Murat himself," Cleo said. "I think you're going to have to solve that one on your own."

Daphne knew she was right. "I appreciate the support."

Billie slipped to the edge of the sofa and leaned close. "I'm about to say something I shouldn't, but I have to because I feel bad about what happened. Cleo, you can't tell anyone. Not Zara or Sadik or anyone."

"I won't. I promise."

Billie nodded and stared at Daphne. "If you want to leave, just tell me. I can get you on a plane and back to the States in five hours."

Daphne thought of the long flight over. "How is that possible?"

Billie grinned. "We'd take a jet. No luggage room, but plenty of speed. I need an hour's notice. That's all. If it gets bad and you need to run, I'll take you."

Daphne felt her eyes start to burn. These women didn't even know her and yet they were willing to offer so much support.

"I appreciate the offer. I doubt things will come to that, but if they do, I know where to find you."

The women left after lunch. Daphne walked into the gardens and admired the bronze artwork there. Her favorite piece stood in the center of a large, shallow pool. A life-size statue of a desert warrior on the back of a stallion. As she studied the power in the horse's flanks and the fierce expression on the warrior's face, her fingers itched to be back in clay. She wanted to make something as wonderful as this.

"If only I had that much talent," she said ruefully. But she still enjoyed the process. She had time for that here. Time for many things she enjoyed.

She sat on a bench and raised her face to the sun. Now that she was alone, she could admit the truth. She missed Murat.

Despite his imperious ways and how he made her crazy, she missed him. She wanted to hear his voice and laughter. She wanted to watch him work and know that his strength would one day be their children's. She wanted his touch on her body and her hands on his.

So when exactly had she stopped hating enough to

start caring about him? Or had she ever hated him? What did she do now? Accept what had happened and move on?

Her heart told her no. That giving in would mean a lifetime of never being more than an object in his life. She wanted more than his rules and wishes. She wanted him to care. To woo her. To love her.

She dropped her chin to her chest as the truth washed over her. She wanted him to love her enough to come after her, instead of always letting her go so easily. She wanted to know it was safe to fall in love with him.

But how? How did she convince a man who believed he was invincible that it was all right to be vulnerable once in a while? How did she get him to open up to her? How did she get him to give her his heart?

She touched her stomach. If she was pregnant, she had her lifetime to figure it out. If she wasn't, then time might be very, very short.

Which did she want? If she had to choose right now, which would it be?

Murat couldn't remember the last time he'd been drunk. He usually didn't allow himself to indulge. As crown prince it was his responsibility to be alert at all times. But tonight he couldn't bring himself to care.

He'd waited all day for Daphne to return, but she had not. Even as he and his people rode deeper into the desert, he watched the sky for a helicopter that did not come.

He should never have ordered the helicopter. He knew that now. If he'd ignored her outburst, she would still be with him. But her reluctance to accept their marriage as something that could not be changed made him furious. How dare she question his authority? He had honored her by marrying her. It was done, and they needed to simply move forward.

But did Daphne see it that way? Was she logical and grateful? No. She constantly fought him, making life difficult, looking at him with accusations in her eyes.

He reached for the bottle of cognac and poured more into his glass. The smooth liquid burned its way down his throat.

Time, he told himself. He had time. Unless she wasn't pregnant. Then she would leave as she had before.

Do not think about that, he told himself. She would not leave again. He wouldn't permit it. Nor would the king.

The sound of muted footsteps forced his gaze from the fire. He watched as several of the tribal elders approached, bowed, then joined him by the fire.

"Will you be attending the camel races tomorrow, Your Highness?" one of the men asked.

Murat shrugged. He had wanted Daphne to see them, but now… "Perhaps. After the morning petitions."

"The council sessions went well today," another said. "Your justice, as always, provides a safe haven for your people."

Murat knew the compliments were just a way to ease into the conversation the old men *really* wanted to have with him. He thought of how Daphne would listen attentively, all the while secretly urging them to get to the point.

She played the games of his office well. She understood the importance of ritual and tradition, even when she didn't agree with it. Unlike many women he had met, she would have patience for tribal councils and diplomatic sessions and negotiations.

"You made an interesting choice with Aisha," the first man said. "To give her to Barak."

He decided to help them cut to the chase. "The decision was a gift to my bride. It was her request that the young lovers be allowed to start a new life."

"Ah." The elders nodded to each other.

"Of course," one of them said, "a woman sees with her heart. It has always been the way. Their tender emotions make them stewards of our households and our children. But when it comes to matters of importance, they know to defer to the man."

Not all of them, Murat thought as he took another drink. He wondered what Daphne would make of being called the steward of his household. The title implied employment and a distance between the parties far greater than in a marriage.

One of the elders cleared his throat. "We could not help but notice the princess has left us. We hope she was not taken ill."

"No. Her health continues to be excellent."

"Good. That is good."

Silence descended. Murat stared into the flames and wished the old men would get to the point, then leave him alone.

"She is American."

"I had noticed that," Murat said dryly.

"Of course, Your Highness. It is just that American women can be strong-willed and stubborn. They do not always understand the subtleties of our ways." The man speaking held up both hands in a gesture of surrender. "Princess Daphne is an angel among women."

"An angel," the others echoed.

"Not the word I would have chosen," Murat muttered. She was more like the devil—always prodding at him. If he wasn't careful, she would soon be leading him around by the nose.

"Have you tried beating her?" one of the men asked.

Murat straightened and glared. The old man shrank back.

"A thousand pardons, Your Highness."

Murat rose and pointed into the darkness. "Go," he commanded. "Go and never darken my path again."

The man gasped. To be an elder and told to never show his face to the prince was unheard of. The old man stood, trembling, then crept away into the night.

Murat sank down by the fire and looked at each of the six remaining men. "Does anyone else wish to suggest I beat my wife?"

No one spoke.

"I know you are here to offer aid and advice," he said. "In the absence of the king, you are my surrogate family. But make no mistake—Princess Daphne is my wife. She is the one I have chosen to be the mother of my children. Her blood will join with mine and our heirs will rule Bahania for a thousand more years. Remember that when you speak of her."

The men nodded.

Murat turned his attention to the fire. As much as Daphne frustrated him, he had never thought to hit her. What would that accomplish? He already knew he was physically stronger. Old fools.

"Do you know why the princess left us?" one of the men asked in a soft, timid voice.

Interesting question. Murat realized he did not know. One minute they had been fighting and the next she was gone.

"She angered me. I spoke in haste," he admitted.

"You could demand her return," a man said.

Murat knew that he could. But to what end? To have her staring at him with anger in her eyes? That was not how he wished to spend his days. Yet to spend them without her was equally unpleasant.

"The prince wishes her to return on her own," another man said.

Murat squinted at him through the flames. He was small and very old. Wizened.

"The elder speaks wisely," he said. "I wish her to return to me of her own accord."

The tiny man nodded. "But she will not. Women are like the night jasmine. They offer sweetness in the shadows, when most of the world slumbers. Other flowers give their scent in the day, when all can enjoy them. A very stubborn flower."

"So now what?" Murat asked.

"Ignore her," one man said. "Give her time to get lonely. She will be so grateful to see you when you do return that she will bend to your will."

An interesting possibility, Murat thought. Although Daphne wasn't the bending type.

"You could take a mistress," another suggested. "One of the young beauties who travel with us. A man does not miss the main course when there are many sweets at the table."

He shook his head. Not only was he not interested in any other woman, he had given his word. He would honor his vows until his death.

"A flower needs tending," the little old man said. "Left alone it grows wild, or withers and dies."

The other elders stared at him. "You wish Prince Murat to go to her? To go after a woman?"

Murat was equally surprised by the advice. "I am Crown Prince Murat of Bahania."

The old man smiled in the darkness. "I do not believe her ignorance about your title and position are at the heart of the problem."

Daphne had said much the same thing.

"The gardener yields to the flower," he continued. "He kneels on the ground and plunges his hands deep in the soil. His reward is a beauty and strength that lasts through the harshest of storms."

The cognac had muddled Murat's brain to the point that the flower analogy wasn't making any sense. "You want me to what?"

"Go to her," the old man said. "Provide her with fertile soil and she will bloom for you."

If Daphne grew anything it would be thorns, and she would use them to stab him.

Go to her? Give in?

Never. He was a prince. A sheik. She was a mere woman.

He reached for the bottle, then stood abruptly and stalked into his tent without saying a word. When he reached the bedroom, he stood in the silence and inhaled the scent of Daphne's perfume.

How he ached for her.

"Go to her," the old man had said.

And then what?

Daphne stood her ground with the servants and basically bullied them into helping her set up her art table and supplies in the garden of the harem.

"But the crown prince said you were not to return here," one of the men said, practically wringing his hands.

"I'm not moving in," she said, trying to be as patient as possible. "I just want to work here. It's quiet, and the light is perfect."

With a combination of prodding, carrying most of the stuff herself and threatening to call the king, she got her supplies in place and finally went to work.

The clay felt good against her bare hands. She had a vision for what she wanted the piece to be, but wasn't sure if her talent could keep pace with her imagination. Sleeplessness made her a little clumsy—she'd spent the past three nights tossing and turning—but she reworked what she had to and kept moving forward with the piece.

The sun had nearly set when she realized she'd had nothing to eat or drink all day. Dizziness made her sink onto the bench in the garden. But the swimming head and gnawing stomach were more than worth it, she thought as she stared at the work she'd accomplished so far. She could—

"I forbade you to come to this place."

The unexpected voice made her jump. She stood and turned, only to see Murat stalking toward her.

"I left specific instructions," he said. "Who allowed you to return to the harem?"

He wore a long cloak over his riding clothes. The fabric billowed out behind him, making him seem even taller and more powerful than she remembered.

She'd missed him. The past seventy-two hours had passed so slowly. Only getting back to her art had kept her sane. She longed to hear him, see him, touch him, but now as he stalked toward her, she wanted to ball up the unused part of her clay and throw it at him.

"I'm not giving you any names," she told him. "And for your information, I'm simply using the garden as my art studio. I can't get the right light in our suite, and the main gardens are too busy. All those people distract me. The harem isn't used, so I'm not in anyone's way."

He glared at her. "You are still living upstairs with me?"

"I was, but I have to tell you, I'm seriously rethinking that decision."

She wiped her hands on a towel and walked away.

Murat watched her go. On the helicopter flight back to the palace, he had thought about all the things he would say to Daphne when he saw her. They had been soft, conciliatory words designed to make her melt into his arms. When she wasn't in their suite, he had gone looking for her, only to be told she was in the harem.

He had thought that meant she had moved back, but he had been wrong. Now what?

He walked out of the garden only to find his father entering the harem. King Hassan shook his head.

"I just passed your wife. She seemed to be very annoyed about something."

"I am aware of that."

His father sighed. "Murat, you are my firstborn. I could not wish for a better heir. You have been born to power and you will lead our people with strength and greatness. But when it comes to Daphne, you seem to stumble at every turn. You must do better. I worked too hard to get her back here and into your life to have you destroy things now."

Chapter Fourteen

Daphne reached the suite she shared with Murat in record time, but once there she didn't know what to do with herself. She wanted to burn off some of the excess energy flowing through her. She wanted to throw something, but everything breakable was far too valuable and beautiful.

After pacing the length of the living room twice, she stopped by the sofa where one of the king's cats slept. Petting a cat or dog was supposed to be calming, she reminded herself. She stroked the animal and scratched under its chin, but still her blood bubbled within her.

"Of all the arrogant, terrible, hard-hearted men on the planet. To think I *missed* him." Talk about stupid.

"Never again," she vowed. "Never ever again will I think one pleasant or kind thought about—"

The door to the suite opened and Murat walked in. She stood and glared at him. "Don't even try to talk to me. I'm furious."

Murat closed the door and walked toward her. "I just spoke with my father."

"Unless you're going to tell me he's agreed to us getting a divorce, I'm not interested."

He unfastened his cloak and draped it across a chair. "He took me to task for annoying you."

"Really? Well, he's a very smart man."

Murat ignored her comment. "He was most disappointed we were not getting along better, especially in light of all his effort to bring us back together."

"I…" She blinked. "What?"

He motioned to the sofa. She sank down next to the cat she'd been petting and waited while Murat sat across from her.

"He told me that he has been waiting a long time for me to pick a bride. When I seemed reluctant, despite the various women in my life, he decided there must be some reason from my past. He made a study of my previous relationships and kept coming back to you and our broken engagement."

"That's right," she said. "Broken and not fixed."

"When he discovered you were unmarried, as well, he decided to bring us back together to see what happened."

"That's not possible." She refused to believe it. "I

wasn't brought here for you. I came because of Brittany…"

She felt her mouth drop open and quickly pressed her lips together. Sensible Brittany who, out of the blue, suddenly decided to marry a man she'd never met and move half a world away.

"She was in on it," she breathed.

"Apparently. No one else in your family knew. My father found out that the two of you were close and contacted her. Together they hatched this plan."

"No." Daphne shook her head. "She would never do that to me. She's not that good a liar."

"Apparently she is." He motioned to the phone. "Feel free to check with her."

"I will." She picked up the receiver and punched in the number for her sister's house. When the maid answered, Daphne asked for Brittany.

"Hey, Aunt Daphne, how's it going? College starts in ten days and I'm *so* excited. Mom's still annoyed with you, but she's getting over it. She thinks I should start dating the governor's son. He's okay, I guess, but not really my type. What's up with you?"

Despite Murat's revelation and the possibility that Brittany had been a part of some plan, Daphne couldn't help smiling as she listened to her niece's monologue.

"I'm good," she said. "I've missed you."

"I've missed you, too. Think I could come over there for winter break? We could go shopping and ride a camel. It would be fun. Plus I'd love to finally meet Murat."

"I'll bet you would. Sure. You can come here. But first I need to ask you something. Did the King of Bahania get in touch with you a couple of months ago?"

Brittany sucked in a breath. "What?"

"Did he want you to pretend to be willing to marry Murat to lure me back to Bahania? Brittany, I want the truth. This is very important."

The teenager sighed. "Maybe. Okay, sort of. Yes. He called and we talked. He was really nice. Not at all like I imagined a king would be. He said that the reason you hadn't fallen in love with any other guy was that you still loved Murat but you wouldn't admit it to anyone. Not even to yourself. At first I told him he was crazy, but then I thought about it for a while and I decided he might be right."

"Oh, God."

"So I said I would marry Murat so that you'd get all worried and stuff. Which you did. I felt bad on the plane. I was acting so shallow, but it was important. And then you went to see Murat and I came home."

"Did anyone else know?"

"Are you kidding? Mom would never have agreed. I sort of felt bad about how excited she got over me marrying a prince and all. But, sheesh, how could she take it seriously? He's so old."

"Practically in his dotage."

"But it worked out great. Right?" Brittany sounded slightly unsure of herself. "I mean you married him and everything. You're happy, Aunt Daphne, aren't you? I'd never hurt you for anything. You know that, right?"

"Of course I know that. I love you, Brittany. You'll always be my favorite niece."

Brittany laughed. "I'm still your only niece, but I know what you mean. How did you find out?"

"The king told Murat."

"Was he furious?"

"He was unamused."

"But you're okay."

Daphne thought about the young woman she'd loved for eighteen years. Whatever Brittany had done, she'd acted out of love and concern.

"I'm completely fine. I love you."

"I love you, too. Let's talk soon."

"Absolutely. Bye."

Daphne hung up the phone and looked at her husband. "It's true. Brittany was a part of it from the beginning. She pretended to be interested in marrying you to get me on the plane."

He leaned back in the chair and closed his eyes. "And I played right into my father's hands by losing my temper and locking you in the harem."

Not to mention marrying her against her will, but she didn't say that.

"I'm pretty mad," Daphne admitted. "But I also feel kind of stupid. I can't believe those two were able to trick us like that."

Murat looked sheepish. "It does not say much about our powers of reasoning. I kept telling my father I was not interested in a teenage bride, but he insisted she be brought over for my inspection."

"I got all maternal and demanding," she said. "I was terrified Brittany was throwing away her life." She glanced at him. "Not that life as your wife is so terrible, but it wasn't right for her."

"Believe me, I did not want her, either."

Daphne felt as if she'd shown up for a big party only to find out the celebration had been the previous night. She felt both awkward and let down.

"So, um, now what?" she asked.

He straightened. "I should not have yelled at you before," he said, "when I found you in the garden. As I told you, I thought you had moved out of our rooms."

Had Crown Prince Murat of Bahania just apologized? "I know. I'm sorry. I didn't mean to give that impression. I just wanted to work with my clay."

"As you should. I enjoy the things you create." He smiled. "Even when they mock me."

Something tightened her heart. She felt happy and nervous at the same time. She cleared her throat.

"I didn't really want to leave. Before. Our trip into the desert. All this is so confusing and I reacted to that and what happened with Aisha. I don't always know what I'm feeling. Then we were fighting, and you said I could go and I said I wanted to and then I was here."

He stood and crossed to the sofa, where he sat next to her. He took both her hands in his.

"I missed you, Daphne. So much so that the tribal elders came to offer me advice."

She liked him touching her, but even more than that, she liked the sincerity in his gaze and that he'd missed her.

"What did they say?"

"One suggested I beat you. I sent him away."

"Thank you. I wouldn't respond well to a beating."

"I am many things, but I am not a bully."

"I know." He would never use his position of strength to take advantage of someone physically.

"One thought I should take a mistress."

Her stomach clenched. The sharp pain made her gasp. "What did you decide?"

He pulled one hand free and touched her cheek. "I want no other woman. Even if I chose not to be bound by my vows, I would still be true."

The pain eased.

"Finally, the oldest of the elders told me you were like a flower and that I should tend you in your garden."

She frowned. "What does that mean?"

"I was hoping you could tell me."

"I haven't a clue."

He stared deeply into her eyes as he slid his hand from her cheek to her mouth. He brushed his fingers against her lips. "Stay with me."

She didn't know if he meant that night or for always. Her heart told her to give in, that in time Murat would learn to yield, while her head reminded her that to stay based on an expected change in behavior was foolish.

Could she accept Murat as he was? Could she be with him knowing he would overrule her at will and never let her be an equal in their relationship? It wouldn't take much for her to fall in love with him again, but would he return those feelings? Could a man who thought of her as a mere woman ever give his heart?

"Stay," he repeated, then saved her from answering by kissing her.

She surrendered to his touch, still not sure how far to hold her heart out of reach.

"You can't be serious," Daphne said over dinner, several days later.

"It will never happen. The Americans are not ready to elect a woman president."

"But if they did…"

Murat shrugged. "You expect me to meet with a woman as an equal?"

"Of course. Didn't your father meet with Prime Minister Margaret Thatcher?"

"Perhaps. I am too young to recall." He cut into his meat. "You seem agitated."

"I'm trying to figure out what I should throw at you."

He raised his eyebrows. "Such threats of violence over a simple discussion. You see why women are not good in politics. There is too much emotion."

She narrowed her gaze, just as she caught the twitch at the corner of his mouth.

"You're toying with me," she said, both relieved and determined to get him back.

"Perhaps."

"I should have known. You *would* meet with a woman president."

"Of course, but I doubt it will happen during my lifetime. Perhaps our son will have to deal with the situation."

She was about to say that any son of hers would respect women and their rights, only to stop herself at the last minute. Perhaps that wasn't the best conversational tack to take. Not when the truce between them was so fragile.

It had been three days since Murat had returned from the desert. Three days in which she'd slept in his bed, made love with him and toyed with the idea of simply accepting her marriage as permanent.

Her feelings grew, and she knew that the point of no return was at hand. If she fell in love with him, she wouldn't want to go, regardless of their past.

"You grow quiet," he said, setting down his knife and fork. "Are you troubled about some matter?"

"No."

Troubled didn't begin to describe her emotions.

"At the risk of starting another battle between us," he said. "It has been nearly three weeks since the first time we made love. You have not started your period."

"I know. I'm late."

She watched him carefully, but his expression didn't change. She wondered if he was crowing on the inside.

"Do you think you are pregnant?"

She wasn't sure. "I don't feel any different, but I don't know if I should. I could get a pregnancy test and take it if you would like."

"What would you prefer to do?"

"Wait a few more days. Sometimes stress upsets my cycle."

She'd certainly had her share of that in the past month or so.

She expected him to insist that she find out that very evening. Instead he nodded. "As you wish."

She couldn't help smiling. "Are you unwell?"

"No. Why do you ask?"

"You never give in on anything."

He sighed. "I am doing my best to nurture the flower in my garden. Do you feel nurtured?"

She held in a laugh. He *was* trying hard. "Nearly every minute of every day."

"Ah. Now you mock me again." He carefully put his napkin on the table and rose. "I think my flower needs a good pruning."

He had an evil gleam in his eye. Daphne stood and started to back away.

"Murat, no."

"You do not know what I have in mind."

"I can tell it's going to be bad. Now stop this. Think of your delicate flower. You have to be nice."

He made a noise low in his throat and started toward her. She shrieked and ducked away. In a matter of seconds he caught her.

In truth, she didn't mind being dragged against him. Even as he pressed his mouth to hers, he caught her up in his arms and carried her into their bedroom.

"What about dinner?" she asked when he set her on her feet next to their bed and reached for the zipper at the back of her dress.

"I am hungry for other things."

* * *

Murat worked through the messages left for him by his assistant. On the one hand he appreciated his new and warm relationship with Daphne. On the other, he found his workdays long and dull when compared with the nights he spent in her company. While his ministers spoke of the oil reserves and the state of the currency-exchange market, he thought of her body pressing against his and the way she cried out his name when he pleasured her.

Things were as they should be, he thought contentedly. She had made her peace with her situation. Now they would grow together as husband and wife. There would be many children and a long and happy life together.

His assistant knocked on the door.

"Come in," Murat called.

Fouad entered with several folders. "The king wishes to change your lunch meeting to this afternoon. It seems he is to dine with Princess Calah."

Murat smiled at the thought of his father having lunch with the charming toddler. "That is excellent. Have the kitchen send up a second meal to my suite. I will dine with my wife."

"Very good, sir." Fouad set the folders on the desk. "I have had a call from our media office. Princess Daphne turned down an interview request from an American women's magazine. They were surprised, as the publication is known for honest reporting. They were interested in making a connection with her, sir, not doing an exposé."

"Perhaps she is not aware that such interviews are welcome. I will mention it to her."

"Yes, sir."

Fouad completed his business and left. Forty minutes later Murat walked into his suite to find the table set for two.

"This is a surprise," Daphne said as she walked into the living room, then crossed the tile floor to kiss him. "A very pleasant one."

"My father and I were to have lunch, but he chose instead to dine with a very attractive young woman. So I took the opportunity to spend some time with you."

Daphne led him to the table. "Calah?" she asked.

"Of course."

"He loves that little girl."

Murat's gaze dropped to Daphne's flat stomach. Did *his* child grow there? So far she had not gotten her period, nor had she offered to take a pregnancy test. He had decided to let her make the decision. If she was with child, he would soon know.

They sat across from each other and spoke about their morning. As she served them each salad, he mentioned the interview with the American magazine.

"You are welcome to speak with them," he said. "I will not forbid it."

"My flower heart trembles at your generosity," she said in a teasing voice.

He pretended to scowl. "I can see I have been too lenient with you."

"Not to worry, Murat. If I had wanted to give the interview I would have. But I wasn't interested."

"Why not?"

Instead of answering, she mentioned that Billie and Cleo were planning a day trip to the City of Thieves and that she wanted to join them.

"Of course Billie wants to fly us there herself, and the king has said that would not be allowed. She's too far along in her pregnancy."

He watched her as she spoke, noting a slight shadow in her eyes.

"Daphne, why did you refuse the interview?"

"It's not important."

Which meant that it was. "I will not rest until you tell me."

She set down her fork. "If you must know, I didn't know what to say. This was for a big bridal issue they're doing in a few months. They're collecting romantic stories from different couples and they wanted to talk about how we met and fell in love. I didn't think it was a good idea to tell them the truth. That you locked me in the harem then married me against my will while I was unconscious. Rather than having to make up something, I declined the interview."

She continued speaking, changing the subject to the upcoming trip to the City of Thieves, but he could not hear her. The impact of what she had said—a bald statement of a truth he knew well—seemed to render him immobile.

For the first time he understood what she had been

trying to tell him all along. That he had held her captive, like a common criminal. Of course the quarters were luxurious and she had not been mistreated in the least, but he had locked her away. Then, knowing she wanted nothing to do with him, he had taken advantage of a medical condition to force her into marriage.

Had he given her the choice, she would have refused him. She would have left. She was not with him because she wanted to be.

The truth sliced through him like a knife. He had always known that she complained about his treatment, but he had told himself it was all simply the meaningless chatter of a woman with too much time on her hands. He had not considered she had cause for her complaints. Had she been a stranger and appeared with her petition while he had been in the desert, he would have freed her from her marriage and locked away the man in question.

The phone rang in the suite. Daphne excused herself to answer it. Murat took advantage of her distraction to leave the table. He indicated he was going back to his office and she nodded. On his way out, he noticed a new clay sculpture on a table.

Two lovers, he thought. Bodies entwined, arms reaching. The sheer passion of the piece took his breath away. It gave him hope. But as he moved closer, he saw the lovers were faceless.

Did she not see him in the role, or did she wish for another man? He knew he pleased her in bed—her body told the tale all too well for him to think otherwise. But was that enough? Did claiming a woman's body mean anything when a man could not lay claim to her mind or her heart?

Chapter Fifteen

Daphne sat alone in the suite and stared out at the perfect view. The light wind had cleared the air enough for her to see all the way to Lucia-Serrat. Two cats dozed next to her on the sofa, their small, warm bodies providing a comforting presence. But it wasn't enough to heal the ache in her heart.

She wasn't pregnant. Proof had arrived an hour before.

She'd suspected, of course. That was why she'd resisted taking a pregnancy test. She hadn't wanted to *know*. She hadn't wanted to have to choose.

Funny how a month ago she would have been delighted with the chance to escape. She would have already had it out with Murat and been busy packing her bags. But now everything was different.

Instead of relief, she felt a bone-crushing disappointment, which told her a truth she'd tried to deny for a long time—she didn't want to go.

Murat wasn't perfect—he would never understand that what he'd done to her was wrong. He would never see her as a partner, but that didn't stop her from loving him. She wanted to be with him, regardless of his faults. She wanted their children to have his strength and stubbornness. She wanted to be a part of his world and his history. She loved Bahania nearly as much as she loved its heir and she didn't want to go.

Since he'd returned from the desert they hadn't discussed their future. No doubt he assumed her silence meant agreement, but that wasn't her way. She wanted to tell him what she'd decided, even if that meant listening to him say how he'd known what was best all along. She wanted to feel his arms around her as he pulled her close and kissed her. She wanted to take him to bed and get started on making their firstborn.

She stood and walked out of the suite with the intent of finding him in his office. But he wasn't there. His assistant said that he had gone for a walk.

Daphne went to the main garden and saw him sitting on one of the stone benches. His shoulders were slumped as he stared at the ground. An air of profound sadness surrounded him.

"Murat?"

He looked toward her and smiled. His expression brightened and the sadness disappeared as if it had never been. In response, her heart fluttered and she wondered how she had ever fooled herself into thinking she didn't love this man with every fiber of her being.

"I've been looking for you," she said as she walked closer.

"You have found me." He shifted to make room for her, then studied her as she sat next to him. He tucked her long hair behind her ear. "As always, your beauty astounds me."

"I'm not all that."

"Yes, you are."

He sounded so serious, she thought, wondering what was going on.

"Unlike many who shine only for a short time," he continued, "you will be beautiful for decades. Even as time steals the luster of your youth, you will gleam like a diamond in the desert."

"That's very poetic and very unlike you." She frowned. "What's going on?"

"I have been sitting here thinking about us. Our marriage."

Her pulse rate increased. "Me, too. I have to tell you something." She paused, not sure how to say it all—that she loved him, that she wanted to stay and make their marriage work. But the words that came out were, "I'm not pregnant."

He didn't react. His gaze never wavered, his hand on her remained still.

"You are sure?" he asked quietly.

"Very." She waited for him to say something else, and when he didn't, she leaned closer. "What's wrong?

Shouldn't you tell me you're disappointed? That we'll be trying again soon?"

He drew in a breath. "I would have. Before. Now I know that this is for the best."

She jerked back as if he'd slapped her. "What?"

"It is for the best," he repeated. "A child would complicate things between us."

"How can they be complicated? We're married."

"In law, but not in spirit. I am sorry, Daphne. I did so much without thinking of you, and there is only one way to make that right. I will set you free."

She couldn't think, couldn't breathe. Confused and sure she must be hearing things, she pushed to her feet and walked across the path.

"I don't understand," she whispered.

He stood. "I was wrong to keep you here against your will, and I was wrong to marry you without your consent. I thought you did not mean your protests, but you did. We cannot have a marriage where you are little more than a prisoner in a gilded cage. I cannot take back what I have done in the past, but I can set it right." He nodded at the ring on her left hand. "You need not wear that reminder any longer. I will speak to the king and arrange for our divorce. You are free to leave whenever you like."

He turned and walked a few feet, then paused. With his back still to her he said, "Take what you like. Clothing, jewels. Any artwork. Consider it compensation for the wrong done to you. There will be a settlement, of course. I will be generous."

Then he was gone.

She made her way back to the bench where she collapsed. Tears poured down her cheeks. She wanted to scream out her pain to the world, but she couldn't seem to catch her breath.

This wasn't happening, she told herself. It couldn't be that Murat had finally figured it all out, only to let her go.

"I love you," she said to the quiet garden. "I want to stay and be with you."

But he'd never offered that. Was it because he didn't think she would be interested, or was it because he didn't care enough about her? Had she been little more than a convenient bride, one easily forgotten?

She wasn't sure how long she sat there grieving for what could have been. An hour. Perhaps two. Then she straightened and brushed away her tears. All along she'd allowed circumstances to choose her path for her. It was time for her to act. She would find Murat and talk to him. If after she explained her feelings for him and her thoughts about staying in the marriage he still wasn't interested, then she would leave. But she wasn't going to give up without a fight.

Once again she went to his office, but he was not there. Fouad, his assistant, shook his head when she asked what time he would return.

"Prince Murat has left the country," he said. "On an extended trip. He is not expected to return for several weeks."

She couldn't believe it. "He's gone? Where?"

"I have his itinerary here, if you would like it."

She took the offered sheet of paper and tried to read the various entries, but the print blurred.

"Wh-when was this planned?" she asked.

Fouad looked sympathetic. "He has been working on it for a few days now, Your Highness. I'm terribly sorry to be the one to tell you about it."

The paper fluttered from her fingers, but she didn't try to pick it up.

He couldn't have left. Not so quickly. She'd just spoken to him a few minutes ago.

"I don't understand. When did he pack? He can't have just left."

"I'm sorry," Fouad repeated.

Daphne forced herself to smile. "You've been very kind. Thank you."

She left and made her way to the elevator, then to the suite she was supposed to share with Murat. Only, he was gone and she was no longer his wife.

She stepped inside to find the king waiting for her.

"My child," he said as he walked toward her. "I have spoken with Murat."

"He's gone," she said, still unable to believe the words. "He left. For several weeks. I had a list of where he was going, but I..." She glanced around for the paper, only to remember she'd dropped it in his office. "He said I could leave. Did he tell you that?"

King Hassan nodded. "The divorce will be finalized as quickly as possible. You are free to return to your life in America."

"Right." Her life. The practice she no longer had, the family who would never forgive her, the friends who couldn't possibly understand what she'd been through.

"He is very sorry for what he has done," the king said. "He sees now that he should never have held you against your will."

She drew in a breath. "Perhaps you shouldn't have meddled, either."

"I agree." Murat's father suddenly looked much older than his years. "I thought the two of you were right for each other. That you only needed time together to realize how right you were. I was an old fool and I hurt you both. I am deeply sorry."

She swallowed, then shook her head. "You weren't wrong. Not completely. I know that Murat isn't interested in me or our marriage, but I…" Her throat tightened. "I love him. I would have stayed." She touched her stomach. "When I told him I wasn't pregnant, he told me to leave."

The king held out his arms, and Daphne rushed into them. She gave in to the tears.

"I could call him back," King Hassan said. "He still has to listen to me."

Temptation called, but she pushed it away.

"Please don't," she said as she straightened and wiped her face. "There has been too much manipulation already. I wouldn't want Murat to be forced into our relationship. I would only want him there because it was what he desired."

"What will you do now?"

"Go back to the States."

The king bent down and kissed her cheek. "Stay as long as you would like. Despite what has happened, you are welcome here."

"I doubt Murat would be thrilled to come home and find me here."

"You never know."

She was pretty sure. He'd let her go without a fight— as he always had.

It took her most of the next day to gather the courage to pack her things and prepare to leave. She only took a few items of the new clothing she'd received since marrying Murat—the things she'd worn in the desert and the nightgowns she'd worn in their bed. She left all the jewelry, including the diamond band that had been her wedding ring.

"Can we do anything?" Billie asked as she hugged Daphne goodbye. "Are you sure you don't want me to fly you home?"

"I think I'll be more comfortable on the king's plane, but thanks."

Cleo moved in for her hug. "I'm sorry Murat is being such a jerk about all this. Men are so stupid." Tears filled her blue eyes. "What I don't get is I would have sworn he was really crazy about you."

Daphne had thought so, too, but she'd been wrong. About so much.

"Keep in touch," Cleo said.

Daphne nodded even though she knew it would never happen. They might send a card back and forth, but in the end they had nothing in common.

"You've both been terrific," she said. "Please tell Emma goodbye for me. And tell Zara and Sabrina I'm sorry I never had the chance to meet them."

The three women hugged again, then Daphne walked out of the suite with them and carefully closed the door behind her.

She rode alone to the airport. Cleo and Billie had offered to come with her, but she wanted to be by herself. She was done with tears and hopes and shattered dreams. She didn't want to feel anything, ever again.

But the burning ache inside of her felt as if it could go on forever. How was she supposed to get over loving Murat? Only now that she had lost him forever did she realize that he had been her heart's desire from the very beginning.

Murat stepped out of the limo and hurried inside the palace. Urgency quickened his steps as he raced up the stairs to the suite he shared with Daphne. He jerked open the door and stepped inside.

"Daphne?"

The large space echoed with silence.

"Daphne? Are you here?"

He walked into their bedroom. She wasn't there. Nor was the book she kept on her nightstand. He moved to the bathroom next and saw her makeup tray was empty. She was gone.

Defeat crashed through him. He had gone away to forget her only to realize that she was with him always. Even knowing that he owed her the choice, he wanted the chance to convince her to stay. But she hadn't even waited two days.

He walked down the hall and into his office. Two things caught his attention at once—a diamond band placed exactly in the center of his desk and the sculpture of the lovers he'd seen before.

He moved forward and picked up the ring. Funny how it still felt warm, as if she had only just removed it. He squeezed it in his hand, then dropped it into his jacket pocket. Then he turned his attention to the clay.

The intense embrace mesmerized him. He followed the graceful line of arms and torso up to the—

His heart froze. No longer were the lovers faceless. She had pressed in features. Just a hint of a nose, a slash for a mouth, but he recognized both of the faces.

Swearing, he picked up the phone and demanded a connection to the airport.

The luxurious jet raced down the runway. Daphne leaned back in the leather seat and closed her eyes. While she doubted she would sleep, she didn't want to watch as Bahania disappeared behind her.

Faster and faster until that moment just before the wheels lifted off. Then the jet suddenly slowed and sharply turned.

"Everything's fine, Your Highness," the pilot said over the intercom. "A signal light came on to tell us the cargo door isn't closed tight. We need to return to the hangar. It will only take a couple of minutes to fix."

She nodded her agreement, then realized the man couldn't see her. "Thanks for letting me know," she said as she pushed the intercom button on the console beside her seat.

She flipped through the stack of magazines left for her and picked out one on interior design. When she returned to Chicago, she either had to join another practice or go out on her own. That had been her plan when she'd left.

Maybe a change in cities would be nice. She'd never lived in the South or the West. She could go to Florida, or perhaps Texas.

She glanced out the window and saw several uniformed crewmen rushing around the plane. Then the main door opened. Daphne looked up in time to see a tall, handsome, imperious man striding on board.

Her heart took a nosedive for her toes. Rational thought left her as hope—foolish hope—bubbled in her stomach.

Murat took the seat opposite hers and leaned toward her.

"How could you leave without telling me you love me?" he demanded.

"I…I didn't think you'd want to know."

He scowled. "Of course I want to know that my wife loves me. It changes everything."

She couldn't think, couldn't breathe, couldn't do anything but drink in the sight of him.

"You told me to leave," she reminded him.

"I thought you were anxious to be gone." He glared at her. "This is your fault for not confessing your feelings." His expression softened. "I am happy to know my love is returned."

She couldn't have been more surprised if he'd told her he was a space alien.

"You l-love me?" she asked breathlessly.

"With all my heart and every part of my being." He took her hands in his. "Ah, my sweet wife. When I realized how badly I had treated you, I did not know how to atone for what I had done. Setting you free seemed only right, even though it was more painful than cutting off my arm. When you accepted my decision without saying anything, I thought you did not care about me."

"I was too shocked to speak," she admitted. "Oh, Murat, I do love you. I have for a long time. Maybe for the past ten years. I'm not sure."

He stood and pulled her to her feet. "You are a part of me. You are the one I wish to be with for always. I want you to share in my country, my history. I love you, Daphne."

She wasn't sure if he pulled her close or she made the first move. Suddenly she was in his arms and he was kissing her as if his life depended on her embrace.

She clung to him, needing him more than she'd ever needed anyone ever.

He pulled back. "But if you must leave, I will let you," he said.

She couldn't believe it. "But you said—"

He smiled. "You may go, but I am coming with you. I will be next to you always."

She laughed. "I don't want to go anywhere. I love Bahania and I love you."

Right there, in the walkway of a jet, Crown Prince Murat of Bahania dropped to one knee.

"Then stay with me. Be my wife, the mother of my children. Love me, grow old with me and allow me to spend the rest of my life proving how important you are to me."

"Yes," she whispered. "For always."

He stood and reached into his jacket pocket. When he withdrew a ring, she started to shake. Then she realized he wasn't holding the diamond band he'd given her after their marriage. Instead he held a familiar and treasured engagement ring—the one she'd left behind ten years ago.

"My ring," she said breathlessly. "You kept it all this time."

"Yes. In a safe place. I was never sure why, until now. I know I was keeping it for you to wear again." He slid on the ring, then kissed her.

Lost in the passion of his body pressing against hers, she barely heard the crackle of the intercom.

"Prince Murat?" It was the pilot. "Sir, are we still going to America?"

"No," Murat said into the intercom. He sank onto a chair and pulled Daphne onto his lap. "We are not."

"Are we going anywhere?"

Murat leaned close and whispered in her ear. "Do

you have any pressing engagements for the rest of the afternoon?"

She shifted so she could straddle him. "What did you have in mind?"

He chuckled, then pressed the intercom button again. "Once around the country."

"Yes, sir."

"Which gives us how long?" she asked.

He reached for the buttons on her blouse.

"A lifetime, my love. A lifetime."

* * * * *

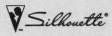

SPECIAL EDITION™

GOLD RUSH GROOMS

Lucky in love—and striking it rich—
beneath the big skies of Montana!

**The excitement of Montana Mavericks:
GOLD RUSH GROOMS continues**

with

PRESCRIPTION: LOVE
(SE #1669)

by favorite author

Pamela Toth

City slicker Zoe Hart hated doing her residency in a
one-horse town like Thunder Canyon. But each time
she passed handsome E.R. doctor Christopher Taylor in
the halls, her heart skipped a beat. And as they began
to spend time together, the sexy physician became a
temptation Zoe wasn't sure she wanted to give up. When
faced with a tough professional choice, would Zoe opt to
go back to city life—or stay in Thunder Canyon with the
man who made her pulse race like no other?

Available at your favorite retail outlet.

Silhouette®
Where love comes alive™

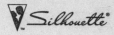

SPECIAL EDITION™

Don't miss the second installment in the exciting new continuity, beginning in Silhouette Special Edition.

THE
F RTUNES
OF TEXAS:
Reunion

A TYCOON IN TEXAS
by Crystal Green

Available March 2005
Silhouette Special Edition #1670

Christina Mendoza couldn't help being attracted to her new boss, Derek Rockwell. But as she knew from experience, it was best to keep things professional. Working in close quarters only heightened the attraction, though, and when family started to interfere would Christina find the courage to claim her love?

**Fortunes of Texas: Reunion—
The power of family.**

Available at your favorite retail outlet.

Silhouette®
Where love comes alive™

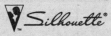

SPECIAL EDITION™

Introducing a brand-new miniseries by
Silhouette Special Edition favorite author
Marie Ferrarella

One special necklace,
three charm-filled romances!

BECAUSE A HUSBAND
IS FOREVER

by Marie Ferrarella

Available March 2005
Silhouette Special Edition #1671

Dakota Delany had always wanted a marriage like
the one her parents had, but after she found her
fiancé cheating, she gave up on love. When her
radio talk show came up with the idea of having her
spend two weeks with hunky bodyguard Ian Russell,
she protested—until she discovered she wanted Ian
to continue guarding her body forever!

Available at your favorite retail outlet.

Where love comes alive™

If you enjoyed what you just read,
then we've got an offer you can't resist!

Take 2 bestselling love stories FREE!
Plus get a FREE surprise gift!

Clip this page and mail it to Silhouette Reader Service™

IN U.S.A.	IN CANADA
3010 Walden Ave.	P.O. Box 609
P.O. Box 1867	Fort Erie, Ontario
Buffalo, N.Y. 14240-1867	L2A 5X3

YES! Please send me 2 free Silhouette Special Edition® novels and my free surprise gift. After receiving them, if I don't wish to receive anymore, I can return the shipping statement marked cancel. If I don't cancel, I will receive 6 brand-new novels every month, before they're available in stores! In the U.S.A., bill me at the bargain price of $4.24 plus 25¢ shipping and handling per book and applicable sales tax, if any*. In Canada, bill me at the bargain price of $4.99 plus 25¢ shipping and handling per book and applicable taxes**. That's the complete price and a savings of at least 10% off the cover prices—what a great deal! I understand that accepting the 2 free books and gift places me under no obligation ever to buy any books. I can always return a shipment and cancel at any time. Even if I never buy another book from Silhouette, the 2 free books and gift are mine to keep forever.

235 SDN DZ9D
335 SDN DZ9E

Name	(PLEASE PRINT)	
Address	Apt.#	
City	State/Prov.	Zip/Postal Code

Not valid to current Silhouette Special Edition® subscribers.

Want to try two free books from another series?
Call 1-800-873-8635 or visit www.morefreebooks.com.

* Terms and prices subject to change without notice. Sales tax applicable in N.Y.
** Canadian residents will be charged applicable provincial taxes and GST.
All orders subject to approval. Offer limited to one per household.
® are registered trademarks owned and used by the trademark owner and or its licensee.

SPED04R

©2004 Harlequin Enterprises Limited

Curl up and have a

Heart *to* Heart

with

Harlequin Romance®

Just like having a heart-to-heart
with your best friend, these stories
will take you from laughter to tears
and back again. So heartwarming
and emotional you'll want to
have some tissues handy!

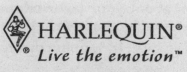